The Correspondent of Petrograd

Another tale of the *sica*.

Jonathan Harries

Rhino Books
An imprint of Jonathan Harries Ink
7 Harrison St 6N
New York, NY 10013

www.jonathanharriesink.com

ISBN (print): 978-1-950628-16-2
ISBN (ebook): 978-1-950628-15-5

First edition

Contents

Foreword

Proof is impartial.

It favors neither truth nor lie but works equitably and determinedly to establish either. Or so a lawyer friend of mine told me the other day after a couple of martinis. But what happens when the proof you seek is elusive? When it hovers like an indecisive hummingbird between the begonias or the dahlias, and no amount of effort spent on research provides sufficient evidence to distinguish fact from fiction, from what happens in real life to what takes place in your head? These are precisely the issues I've faced in my exploration into the history of my family's nearly 2000-year-old assassination business.

If you've read *The Tailor of Riga*—my first incursion into the highly dubious history of what the famed but unscrupulous archaeologist Dr. Jacob Peretz termed "the most immoral family that ever fouled the earth" (rude bastard)—you'll understand my dilemma. Peretz wrote this slight in a threatening letter to me shortly after he'd translated the story of our family's origins from a previously undiscovered Dead Sea Scroll he'd found in the Caves of Qumran in the Judean Desert.

As I told him just before his untimely demise (poor fellow tripped in the shower, smashed the glass door and severed his hepatic artery), "Just because one's ancestors have been taking out reprobates since the first Jewish uprising against the Romans in AD 70, it doesn't mean they're contemptible."

Both his notes and the scroll mysteriously vanished shortly after his death and haven't been seen since. Of course, I still had the stories passed on to me by my father and mother on my seventeenth birthday together with the razor-sharp daggers known as *sicae*—the millennia-old tools of our trade—to go on. And it was from these that I wrote the first book in the saga, *The Tailor of Riga.* In it you can learn the history of both the Isakowitsch (my father's line) and Smulian (my mother's) families. How they were kicked out of the Tribe of Asher in ancient Israel by the Levites for breaking more of the commandments than their neighbors and cursed to carry out assassinations for seventy generations. It only takes up a page or two at the beginning of the book, but it is the foundation upon which everything you're about to read about us is built.

A few months after *The Tailor of Riga* was published in May 2020, I received a mysterious package from an unknown relative in Argentina with what she called "the notes" of an ancestor on my mother's side who'd gone to India from Baghdad in 1858 on behalf of the Maharajah of Kutch. His mission was to assassinate a British officer, whose brutality against the survivors of the Great Sepoy Rebellion was positively sickening, and to retrieve a priceless ruby pendant and emerald necklace that the swine had stolen. While the notes of Elliot Smulian-

Hasson provided further plausibility to the story, as far as I was concerned they still fell short of the absolute proof I needed.[1]

As is usually the case, once the proverbial ball gets rolling, things begin to pop out of the woodwork faster than you can blink. While the story of how my great-uncle Leon became the bodyguard to the second White Rajah of Sarawak didn't exactly "pop out the woodwork," it was found between the pages of an old book he'd left me in his will, *The Adventures of Haji Baba of Ispahan*.[2]

Part two of Leon's diary was discovered by my son Simon a month later in an envelope hidden between the cover and endpaper of volume three of The Haji Baba saga. It covers Leon's activities in Europe from 1912 to1914 and then his part in the death of the Russian mystic Rasputin in1916. As in *The Bodyguard of Sarawak*, Leon had written the second part of his diary in the third person, as if he intended it to become a novel. I'm not sure why he didn't publish it during his lifetime. It wasn't as if he lacked the time. He lived until he was eighty-six, and other than reading from his vast collection of books and carousing with various female friends, he didn't—as far as I knew—do much of anything.

My only thought is that what he'd written in part two— and what I've called *The Correspondent of Petrograd*—

---

[1] You can read about Elias' exploits in *The Carpet Salesman from Baghdad*, the second volume in the tales of the sica.

[2] Once again you can find the first part of great-uncle Leon's escapades detailing his work for the British Secret Service Bureau in 1912 in Kenya, Singapore, and Sarawak, in *The Bodyguard of Sarawak*.

about the events in London, Vienna, Hamburg, Schwerin, and Petrograd was still classified under the Official Secrets Act. It may still be for all I know. I tried to call MI6 in London, but the person who answered the phone told me that Covid restrictions were still in effect and that she was sure someone would contact me at some stage. I waited a few months, and when I didn't hear anything I decided to go ahead and publish the book.

I'm not a big risk taker, but my feeling is that MI6 is not overly concerned with what happened a hundred years ago with everything else they're dealing with these days. So, just to be clear, what you're about to read may very well still be classified. If you're of a nervous disposition, you'll want to delete the book from your Kindle or burn the paperback. However, if you're made of sterner stuff, then I hope you enjoy the story. It begins the morning after Leon's return to Singapore from Sarawak on his way back to London. He'd had a troubling dinner with the man known as C., Leon's contact at MI6, the evening of his return followed by a highly demanding session of lovemaking with the beautiful Lily Tan.

Chapter 1 — 1912 Singapore and London

Old endings and new beginnings

As agreed, Leon met Captain Mansfield Smith-Cumming, head of the foreign section of the British Secret Service Bureau, for breakfast in the Tiffin Room of Raffles Hotel in Singapore. The purpose of the meeting was for Leon to give C. (as he insisted on being called) his final answer on taking the Serbian assignment that had been proposed at dinner the previous evening.

Leon found C. sitting at a corner table reading a copy of *The Singapore Free Press* and *Mercantile Advertiser*. He looked up when he saw Leon and unscrewed his monocle.

"You know what I like about breakfasts in this part of the world?" C. pierced a slice of pineapple with his fork and waved it at Leon. "The fruit. You can of course get pineapple back home, but it doesn't taste the same. This stuff is plucked off whatever type of foliage pineapples are plucked off every single day, I'm told by the waiter. It's bloody marvelous, I tell you." He picked up a bowl of sliced mango and handed it to Leon. "Here, have some

1

mango, dear boy, before I scarf every piece of fruit the hotel has to offer."

"Thank you, C., perhaps I shall in a few minutes. Right now, I need to give you my decision as it pertains to last night's conversation."

"You sound very formal this morning. Never a good sign in my experience, but do go ahead. I'm all ears," C. said, putting down his fork with the remnants of the pineapple still attached and screwing his monocle back in. "I trust I'm not going to be disappointed?"

"I sincerely hope not. I am going to take the assignment—"

"But?"

"I would like to go home for a few weeks to see my parents. I know you said this couldn't wait, but it's been two years since I saw them last, and I don't know when, or if, I'll get to see them again. They're old."

"Everyone's old compared to you. What are you now, twenty?"

"Yes, but...."

C. waved aside whatever Leon was about to say. "Very well, I suppose it's the least I can do for your family. You know, I've never met your pater, Abraham, but I've seen the files on how he took care of Amir Bregu, the Albanian killer that all of London knew as Jack the Ripper. They're impressive. And of course, your brother Joe, who killed Jörg Grunewald, the German spymaster. You and your family have provided invaluable service to His Majesty's Government over the past twenty-two years."

"I appreciate that."

"In any case, I may have spoken a little hastily last

night when I said Europe's needs were more important than your own. As it turns out it, we've bought ourselves a little time."

"How? Last night you were adamant that a massive war was imminent."

"It still is, but I received correspondence this morning from our people in the Balkans that Serbia, Bulgaria, and Greece together with the Montenegrins are about to declare war on the Ottoman Empire. Take a look." He showed Leon an article in the newspaper headed "Troubled Balkans." "It's even mentioned in the damn press out here already. Our Black Hand friend, Colonel Dragutin Dimitrijević, has been made head of Serbian Intelligence, so any plans he has of instigating war with the Austro-Hungarian Empire will no doubt be on hold until the Balkan unpleasantry is resolved. It's a complete mess. The Serbians are greedy bastards and the new Turkish regime—they call themselves 'The Young Turks'—are a disorganized rabble. And don't get me started on the Albanian Hamidian revolutionaries."

"Have no fears in that regard," Leon said under his breath, hoping C. wasn't going to drone on about what was happening in the Balkans. As far as he was concerned, they could all blow each other to hell, and the less he knew the better. "Well, in that case, if it's all the same to you, I'll probably hang around London for a month or so to see my parents. Then, if you don't need me, maybe head back to South West Africa. My brother was awfully keen for me to return the *sica*."

"Fair enough, but hold off on scuttling back to Africa until you do hear from me. I'll be back in London in a few weeks. Someone from our office will inform you of arrangements."

Later that evening Lily Tan, head of C.'s Singapore division, took Leon to the docks in her Bugatti Type 13 to board the steamship *Arratoon Apcar* for his trip back to London via Bombay. She looked positively radiant despite a night of strident copulation in which she'd put Leon through his paces to see if he remembered all he'd learned in the three rooms of the Heavenly Abode of the Crimson Lotus.

"When will I see you again, Lily?" There was a note of desperation in Leon's voice. He'd fallen hard for Lily, harder than he'd fallen for any other woman, and the thought of leaving her was tearing at him.

Lily picked up on Leon's funk immediately. She gave him a sympathetic smile. "I doubt if we will see each other again, Leon. It doesn't work like that in our business. But you can leave knowing that I enjoyed my time with you."

"Just enjoyed?" he asked, sounding hurt.

"Poor, diffident Leon," she replied, patting his cheek. "Don't read too much into everything you hear. I am not someone who uses superlatives often. Let's just say you satisfied me...which few men before you have managed to do. There, do you feel better?"[3]

---

[3] *Editorial note: Leon didn't mention whether he felt better or not, nor did he say much about the three-week passage back to England other than that he was bored out of his mind. Much to his horror, C. had only sprung for a second-class ticket, which put him in a sour mood. Since leaving Cape Town for Mombasa, Bombay, Singapore, and finally*

The Sir Sydney Smith Pub at 22 Dock Street in Whitechapel—proprietor Abraham Harris, purveyor of J&J Vickers Blended Irish Whiskies and Celebrated Gold Medal Gin, and Truman, Hanbury, and Buxton beer—looked the same as it had when Leon had left for South West Africa two years before. The old soot-encrusted lantern still hung from under the Truman sign. The gold leaf on the window still peeled in places, and other than the drapes in the second story window that looked as if they'd been replaced, nothing had changed.

Leon glanced up, hoping to see his mother's face looking down as she had two years before when he'd waved her goodbye before heading for the docks. The drapes fluttered slightly as he watched the window, but it was only the breeze.

He took out his Tissot pocket watch and saw that it was just after noon. Unless things had changed dramatically, the pub would be empty at this hour. Most of its customers didn't drink on their lunch break, preferring instead to get hammered after finishing work. As most patrons worked in butcher shops or garment factories where a slip of the wrist could leave one

---

Sarawak, the Secret Service Bureau had provided first-class accommodation as befitting someone posing as the part owner of a diamond mine. But now he was back to being plain old Leon Harries, son of a pub keeper and jumped-up barrow boy, as one of Rajah Charles Brooke's assistants had reminded him. Clearly there were no extracurricular activities available aboard the ship, or no doubt Leon would have mentioned them. The story picks up again when he arrives in London.

digitally impaired, it was good thinking on their part. Leon knew this was the time his parents would probably be cleaning up last night's mess. He had considered sending them a telegram from Bombay to say he'd be back in a few weeks but decided to surprise them instead.

"We're closed," said Abraham in his heavily accented English. He was polishing the beer taps and didn't even bother to look up at the person at the door who clearly could not read the "Closed until 5pm" sign. Bryna, Leon's mother, did and dropped the enormous jar of pickled eggs she was carrying from the kitchen, shattering the container and sending the foul-smelling eggs all over the floor.

"Oy Gutt!" she yelled in Yiddish. "The bubala is back."

"Leon!" said Abraham, almost leaping from behind the bar in excitement. There was a slight quiver in his normally calm, steady voice. "Welcome home, *boychik.* Come here." He held open his arms and embraced his youngest son before handing him over to his sobbing mother.

"You're thinner," she said, stroking his face. "I'm going to make you something to eat."

Leon hugged her and laughed. "So long as it's not these eggs…here, let me help you."

The three of them cleaned up the reeking remains of what some patrons thought of as dinner and then repaired to the living quarters on the floor above where, over steaming bowls of matzo ball soup and corned beef sandwiches, Leon told his parents about his adventures since leaving London.

Abraham, who was now in his sixties and still looked as

if he could stop a charging buffalo with his bare hands, interrupted Leon just as he got to the redacted version of why he'd had to leave Walvis Bay in a hurry (the last thing Leon wanted his mother to know was that he'd been hounded out by a group of angry husbands hell-bent on doing him mischief on learning of his frequent entanglements with their wives). "Before you go any further," said Abraham, "I know that Joe passed the *sica* on to you. So, no need to hide anything about what happened."

Leon reached down and pulled the curved dagger from the scabbard on his left ankle and placed it on the table. "Here, Dad, maybe you should have it back."

"Oy," Bryna said, throwing a napkin over it, "I thought I'd seen the last of that thing."

"Put it back in its scabbard, my boy. You can't return the *sica*. It can only go down the line, not up. I'm not sure Joe should have given it to you, and I wasn't happy to learn he had. But I suppose you're nearly twenty years younger than him, so maybe that's okay."

"Why? Because of the curse? Joe mentioned that, but it sounds a little farfetched."

"Curse-shmurse," Bryna said. "That's just an old *bubba maisa*. What the family does and why they do it has nothing to do with the evil eye. Maybe people believed it back when we were still tramping through the desert on our way out of Judea, but today it's a commercial enterprise. Nothing more. Your father's too old to take on any new assignments. If you hand the *sica* back to him, then the business is over. So, either keep it or give it back to Joe for his son. I should be that lucky that he gives me a grandson."

Leon picked up the *sica* and looked at it. "I'm not sure I really want to keep it. I told Captain Smith-Cumming that I was going to return it to Joe, and he said to wait until he contacted me. But I can't imagine I'd ever get to use it here in London."

"You never know," replied Abraham. "It came in handy in the Amir Bregu business."

"Ah, yes," said Leon, holding up his finger as if to make a point. "While we're on the subject of business, C., as Smith-Cumming insists on being called, by the way, mentioned that our fees are paid into a Swiss bank account."

"Smith-Cumming...." Abraham said, giving his impressive mustache a twirl. "I just heard that name. He's one of the new boys, isn't he?"

"I don't really know," replied Leon, "but I met him in Mombasa and then again in Singapore just before I left for London. He mentioned that the department was newly formed, but when exactly that was, I'm not sure." He shrugged and took a bite of his sandwich.

Abraham put down his spoon and looked up at the ceiling for a moment, moving his head back and forth as if he were searching through a file cabinet. "Yes, yes. Now I remember. My old contact William Melville told me that they'd reorganized the Secret Service Bureau a year or two ago. A man named Kell, whom he works with, runs the home section and your friend Smith-Cumming the foreign section."

"I doubt he'd call me a friend, but he seemed pleased with the job I did. He said that he was going to get me some sort of commendation."

"And why would he not be pleased?" asked Bryna. "Of

course he should be pleased. I'm sure you did a wonderful job."

"Not just one, Mama." Leon told his parents about his first assignment to assassinate Count Orlov aboard the SS *Gwalior*, omitting only his dalliance with Madame Marie de Pardaillan de Gondrin so as not to upset his mother. He followed this up with the assassinations of Baron Alexander Krissendorff and Philip Krause, members of the Thunder Eagles, a dissident group of Russian and German aristocrats and American industrialists trying to break Russia's treaty with the United Kingdom and France.

"That's impressive for your first time," said Abraham. "Joe said he suspected you'd be a natural."

"Well, there's more," Leon said, feeling quite pleased with himself. He proceeded to tell them how he'd exposed Gubbins, the double agent, saved Rajah Charles Brooke's life, and destroyed the covert group of American imperialists in the jungle outside of Kuching.

"My God," said his father, "I believe you may be the most successful assassin in the history of those of us who've used the Isakowitsch *sica*. No wonder they want to give you a commendation. But I doubt that'll happen. We don't get recognized, just paid."

"Talking of which," said Leon, "you still haven't answered my question about the Swiss bank account. I may need to draw on some funds. I'm pretty depleted in the cash department."

"Yes, by rights part of that is yours. I haven't spoken to our banker lately, but I did get a telegram to say His Majesty's Treasury transferred a substantial amount into our account two weeks ago. That's when I telegraphed Joe to see what he'd been up to. In his reply he mentioned he'd given you the *sica*. But I have to say I had no idea how prolific you were." He reached over and slapped Leon on the back. "I'm proud of you, *boychik*."

His mother, too, reached over and squeezed his hand. "As am I, darling. But I don't like to hear how dangerous all of this was, and I'm surprised the headhunters in Sarawak could resist this handsome head." She squeezed his cheeks until Leon pulled back.

"No need to worry, Mama. My impression from the chief is that headhunters are less concerned about what you look like—only that you have a head. And that's only when they need one for whatever purpose they take heads for. At that moment he didn't need mine. Overall I suppose I had some narrow escapes, but I'm sure that's part of the job."

"Unfortunately, it is," replied his father. "Most of our family seem to have escaped with only minor injuries every now and then. Nothing life-threatening yet. Now, let's get you settled in. You can have your choice of bedrooms, by the way. When Bessie left for South Africa, we officially became empty nesters."

"I've haven't heard that expression," Leon said, "but it's a good one." He reached into his jacket pocket, took out the notebook he'd been keeping since leaving Singapore, and wrote it down.

"What, are you a writer now?" asked Abraham. "Be careful if you're making notes about the business."

"I like writing, and in Sarawak my cover was as an author writing an adventure novel. Don't worry, I haven't put down anything compromising. Yes, Joe told me Bessie had moved to South Africa with her husband I'm sorry I missed her."

"You'll see her and your other sisters if you go back. They're all there now. And then one day hopefully we'll visit and get to see all of you before we die," said Bryna.

"Don't talk like that, Mama. You're both still young and healthy. I'm sure everyone will come back to see you."

"Travel's expensive...."

"Which brings me back to the elusive Swiss Bank account."

"The problem with our Swiss bank account," Abraham said, wiping his mouth with his napkin, "is that it's a numbered account, and the only people who know the number are your mother and me. Even if I gave it to you, I'd have to take you there and introduce you to Herr Meier, who together with two other people at Clariden Leu—that's our bank—know our identity."

"I've got the time."

"You've just got here and already you want to leave?" sighed Bryna.

"No, Mama. That's not what I mean. We could get to Zurich and be back here in a few days. It'll be fun."

Abraham shrugged his huge shoulders. "Fun it might be, but who will run the pub?"

Leon shook his head. "I could really do with the money. Anything the Secret Service Bureau handed me for expenses is gone. All I have left of any value are the fancy clothes they gave me to wear in the first-class dining room. I suppose I can sell them and the robe the Rajah gave me, which he said was worth a lot. I'm just unsure why you're being hesitant with the money. Part of it is mine."

"You're right," Abraham said. "And if that's what you want to do then we'll do it. But—"

"Just tell me," Leon said, trying his best not to sound exasperated.

"Well, there's a lot of money in the account. Enough for you, Joe, and your sisters to start a new life somewhere if things become dangerous in the places you eventually live."

"God forbid," Bryna said. "But our families, like most of the Jews in Europe, have been forced out of just about any country we've settled in. Your father and I always wanted that money to be there in case the same things—the pogroms—began again."

"I understand, but surely we're safe in England and South Africa. Even the Jews in Germany are fine."

"Perhaps, but your grandparents thought we were all safe in Lithuania and Belarus."

"Maybe you're overthinking this."

"You could be right," his father said before pausing. "Let me propose an alternative, and let's say it's just for one year."

"I don't understand."

"Your mother and I make enough money from the pub to live as comfortably as we could ever want. We've got money set aside if we should get sick and have to sell or if anything else should go wrong."

"And I don't want to take your money. You've given me enough over the years."

Abraham held up his hand. "Wait here while I get

something." He stood up from the table, gave Bryna a mysterious look, and disappeared down to the bar. A few minutes later he staggered up the stairs carrying a metal chest the size of a whisky crate. He put it on the table, and Bryna took a key attached to a thin silver chain she wore around her neck and unlocked it.

Abraham opened the lid and then stood back so Leon could look inside. He immediately understood why his father had staggered under the weight. Inside, neatly arranged in wooden compartments, were stacks of gold coins. He had no idea how many, but there must have been hundreds. Another compartment, even larger than those that held the coins, was filled with both uncut and cut gemstones.

"Good grief," Leon said, reaching in and picking up a large sapphire, "what is all this?"

"One of the only side benefits of being an assassin for the Tsar's secret service, the Okhrana, was that we got to keep what was on the people we had to take out," Abraham said. "Some were poor revolutionaries who had very little. Others were wealthy aristocrats who had fortunes. From the poor we took nothing, but from the rich we took everything. At first it felt like stealing, but our pay was so low that we were given permission by Pyotr Rachkovsky, our boss, to keep what we killed. Or should I say, keep whatever those we killed had. Of course, we had to give him a cut, but still I managed to keep most of it. I made the same arrangement with the British Secret Service Bureau at the beginning until I decided that the Swiss bank account was safer."

"There must be a fortune in here," Leon said,

examining some of the gold coins.

"We don't know what everything's worth," Bryna said as she rearranged a stack of gold rubles that had fallen over into a compartment that held British sovereigns. "We've never had the diamonds or sapphires valued, but they're all genuine. That much I know."

"You can take whatever you need from here for expenses, and then I think you should discuss with Smith-Cumming to pay you half up front and the rest into the Swiss bank account on completion of the job. Even half of our normal fee should last you a while. Then in a year or so—depending on how things stand—Joe, you, and I can make the decision about what we want to take from the Swiss account."

Leon picked up a few more of the gold coins, examined them closely, and then put them back into their piles. Both his parents looked at him expectantly.

"I love you both so much," he said, putting his arms around them. "As I've said my whole life, you've given me everything that I need."

"Your whole life?" said Bryna with a dismissive sigh. "You're only twenty...."

"I know, but I really feel I need to try to make my own money. You've got the pub, Joe has the shipping business, my sisters thank goodness are all married or working, but I'm nothing at this point."

"You're nothing?" asked his father. "You're making a joke, surely. Over a period of thirty years, I may have assassinated perhaps fifty people. Joe's only eliminated one or two. You, my boy, have taken out six people...if we don't count the two priests and that man Fish, whom you say the headhunters took care of. And you've done it in a matter of months. Who knows what your body count will be when you go to the Balkans?"

"If I go to the Balkans. C. says the war going on there between the Serbians, Bosnians, Greeks, and Ottomans could last a while. If that's the case, I'm going to need to do something here while I wait."

"You can always assist me here in the pub. We have two waitresses to help your mother, but could use someone else behind the bar."

"Two waitresses, you say?" Leon's ears perked up.

"Yes," replied his mother, who immediately caught Leon's drift. "But don't go getting any ideas. They get distracted enough by the customers."

"Well, look," said Leon, closing the metal case. "I'll help you out behind the bar, but I'm going to see if I can sell that Chinese robe that the Rajah gave me. If it's what he said it was, then it's probably worth a ton, and I can use that to set myself up in some sort of business. Not sure what, but I'll look around. If not, I'll use some of this." He gave the case a tap and smiled at his parents.

"Fair enough," said his father.

"Keep your hands off the waitresses," said his mother.

Chapter 2 – 1913 London

New friends, new job, old skills

On the suggestion of Abraham, Leon took his Chinese robe to Philip Sassoon, whose father, Sir Edward Albert Sassoon, had been a client, though Abraham wasn't prepared to give Leon any information about his assignment from the extremely wealthy, recently deceased politician.

"There's no reason for you to know the details. All you need to understand is that there's a bond between our families. Now that Albert is dead, Philip's in charge, and while he's young—not much older than you—he's very worldly. If anyone can put you in touch with the right person to sell the robe, it's Philip Sassoon. He's the best-connected person in London these days."

Leon had only heard the name Sassoon from articles he'd read in the papers. He knew the family was immensely wealthy and that Philip's mother had been a Rothschild. Abraham set up the meeting, and at four o'clock on a Tuesday afternoon, Leon went to the Sassoon mansion at 25 Park Lane. An immaculately attired butler showed him to the drawing room, where Philip Sassoon was waiting to greet him.

If Leon was expecting a stuck-up prig, he was pleasantly surprised. Philip could not have been more welcoming and friendly. They were, as Abraham had said, both about the same age, and yet Philip seemed older, as if he'd already given up on his youth. As the scion of two famous families, Philip was more than a level above Leon's East End roots, and yet his manner was genial and sincere. When his butler had poured them both a cup of tea, Philip asked Leon how he could help.

"Before I tell you, I'd like to offer my deepest condolences on the recent death of your father," Leon said. Abraham had told him that Philip's father, Sir Edward Sassoon, had died just a month before.

"Thank you," said Philip. "That's most kind of you. He died young, but I believe his was a life well lived. I shall soon take his seat in Parliament, though I have little desire to do so. But, obligations etcetera, etcetera. *Absens haeres non erit* as my Latin teacher once said "

"I'm afraid Latin was not in my syllabus," Leon replied, feeling quite stupid in the presence of such an erudite and sophisticated figure.

"It means an absent person will not be an heir. If I didn't agree to take his seat, the old man would have had second thoughts about my inheritance." He laughed. "Fortunately, my mother's side of the family is where the real money lies. I jest, of course. But enough about me. You, too, have led quite an interesting life, your father tells me. Working for His Majesty's government in Kenya and then serving as a bodyguard to the Rajah of Sarawak?"

"Yes, I had the honor of serving him for a short period."

"You did a lot more than that, I believe. I met him, you know—the Rajah I mean." said Philip, offering Leon a cigarette which he refused. "Wise man, though I do enjoy them so." He placed one in an ebony holder, lit it, and took a long draw. "Anyway, Rajah Charles once came to our house in Trent Park to visit my mother, who was French and had the most marvelous collection of French literature. The man's a Francophile of the first water."

"That he is," Leon said. "And I say that from firsthand experience. I took him a book signed by an author I met onboard a ship from Cape Town to Mombasa. The author actually inscribed the book to me, but he left my name off, and so I told the Rajah it was meant for him. A lie, but he appreciated it more than I would have." He laughed and Philip smiled.

"It's probably a capital offence to lie to a king, but ultimately if the lie makes someone else happy, then what's the harm?"

"My only concern is that the Rajah wants to visit Marcel Proust—that was the writer's name—in Paris when he returns to England at the end of the year. And then I suppose neither will talk to me again."

"Did you say Marcel Proust?" asked Philip, raising his eyebrows.

"Yes, as I said, we met aboard a ship."

"Good Lord, I didn't know the man ever left Paris. He has quite the life there, you know."

"So, he told me...." Leon would have mentioned Proust's share in the Hotel Marigny, the famed male brothel, but decided to hold back until he was better acquainted with Sassoon. "Marcel told me he'd never in a million years have embarked on a cruise, but his doctor recommended he do so for his chest ailment. Eccentric fellow, but I liked him."

"Oddly enough, I know him too. Met him in Paris. Well, well, what a delicious coincidence. You'll have to tell me more. Perhaps we can do dinner one night."

"That's awfully kind of you," replied Leon. "I'd like that very much." He couldn't believe how charming Philip was and how much at ease he'd put him. "Now, I know you're busy, and I don't wish to take up too much of your time."

"Please," replied Philip, waving aside Leon's offer. "Take as much time as you need." He pointed to the oilskin package Leon had carried in. "I imagine whatever's inside that package is what you'd like my advice on?"

Leon unwrapped the package and pulled out the yellow satin robe embroidered with dragons and flowers that Rajah Charles Brooke had given him as a reward for his service to Sarawak.

"My God," said Philip, leaning forward and running the fabric between his fingers. "I know a little of Eastern art, but I don't need to know much to tell you that this is magnificent."

"According to the Rajah," said Leon, reaching to the side pocket of the robe and pulling out a thick cream manila envelope, "and he's written it in this note to me on his letterhead, the robe belonged to Prince Gong, a member of the Qing Dynasty. It was a gift to his uncle, the Rajah James Brooke."

"Hmm," said Phillip as he continued to examine the robe. "I've certainly heard of Prince Gong. He negotiated the Convention of Beijing with the British, French, and Russian leaders after we'd virtually destroyed the place during the Second Opium War. If this is genuine—and who would dare doubt the word of the White Rajah of Sarawak—it must be worth a fortune."

"That's what the Rajah told me, and the truth is I'd like to sell it to set myself up in business."

Philip Sassoon looked at him oddly. "I don't understand—aren't you already in the family business?"

"What do you mean?" asked Leon, starting to feel anxious. He had no idea what Philip knew or didn't know about what the descendants of Jacob ben Yitschak—later Isakowitsch, even later Harris, and then finally Harries—actually did. Abraham had been evasive when Leon had asked what he'd done for Philip's father, but clearly Philip knew more than Leon felt he should.

"You're concerned," said Philip. "I can see that in your face. But I assure you there's no need for us to keep secrets from each other." Philip gave Leon a reassuring smile. "I'm not sure what your father revealed to you about the family relationship? Although knowing him, I suspect very little."

"Virtually nothing," Leon replied, feeling miffed at his father. "Your father obviously had more faith in you than mine does in me."

"Fathers try their best to protect their children. Don't forget my father was dying. He had no choice but to tell me everything he thought I'd need to know. The point is my family's been using yours for years and years. My father told me how he and my grandfather had engaged your father Abraham when they needed his specialized services. In fact, my grandfather said—and this could well be apocryphal— that his father had brought a member of another branch of your family to Bombay from Baghdad to perform some service for him. Said he met your distant relative...an Elias-something-or-other...at his father's house."[4]

When Leon looked up, he became aware that Philip was studying him. It was in the manner a greedy schoolboy might study a jam tart. Leon felt slightly uncomfortable until he realized that Philip's eyes, which were soft and almost sensual, displayed not a hint of malice or judgement. Leon began to relax, but he was still unsure how to respond. Philip stood up and walked over to the window. He stared out at the traffic on Park Lane for a moment and then turned to Leon.

"I doubt very much, Leon, that I will ever have need of your services, but I feel an affinity for you, as if we have known each other for a long time. We are descended from families that have been connected in some manner for generations. We are both of a faith that has struggled for acceptance, and while I have led a life perhaps more privileged than your own, I don't see that as a barrier, and I hope you won't either."

---

[4] *Editorial note: This refers to Elias Smulian-Hasson and the story covered in* The Carpet Salesman of Baghdad. *The hint of two separate-though-related families, each in the same business, came as a bit of a shock to me. I'd always understood that the first time the sica of each branch of the family—separated around the time of the Second Jewish Revolt in about 132 CE against the Romans—was mentioned, was in 1946 when my mother (a descendant of the Ben Shmuel then Smulian) married my father. It was the only occasion in nearly 2000 years that both sicae were in the same place.*

It was an odd statement, Leon thought, and it would have been condescending and arrogant had it come from anyone else. But there was something about Philip, an almost ethereal quality, that made him approachable rather than contemptuous. Leon put down his teacup and walked over to the window where Philip stood.

"Thank you," he said. "I was not expecting that from someone like yourself."

"And what exactly does that mean?" Philip turned to him.

"Over the past few months, I've met a lot of people who've looked down at my, shall we say, humbler background."

"Humbler, perhaps, but intriguing, nonetheless. You have an air about you, Leon. I can't quite put my finger on it, but you are a very appealing young man."

"Thank you," Leon said, going quite red. "Well, I'm glad you know a little about my family. It means I don't have to lie to you, which will be a change. Over the past few months, I've had to pretend to be what I'm not. And I haven't always succeeded. But only three people who saw through the charade accepted me for what I am. Proust, the Rajah, and now you."

Philip laughed. "We shall just have to see whether we can work on that so that no one sees you for anything other than what you are: a decent chap. Or if they do, it's at their peril."

"I'd rather it wasn't at their peril, which is why I'd like to extract myself from the family business as such and set myself up in something else."

"Then I shall help you. Now, I think what we should do

with the robe is take it to Christie's. I know the chairman, and if anyone can tell you its value, it is he."

Later that evening during a lull in the bar's activities, Leon asked Abraham why he hadn't told him that Philip knew about the family business.

"I suspected the two of you would get on, but I wasn't positive. I've known him since he was a small child, and I spent a lot of time with his father. A bit of a snob, but I enjoyed his company. I had no idea that Philip knew the real connection between me, his grandfather, and father until I telephoned him to ask if he'd see you. It was only then that he told me his father had included in his will a note with instructions should Philip ever need our services."

"That explains it, but not why he immediately seemed to take to me."

"I think Philip is deep down a lonely man. He has so-called friends and plenty of them. From dukes and politicians to poets and playwrights. But he is a Jew, and I think few of his acquaintances can ever get over that fact. And Philip knows it."

Leon forgot to ask his father about the other branch of the family that David Sassoon, Philip's great-grandfather, had engaged in Bombay, and over the next months he was so busy that it totally slipped his mind.

The robe which Christie's labelled "An imperial yellow embroidered satin Twelve Symbol robe belonging to the late Prince Gong of the Qing Dynasty" went for a record price. After paying the commission and taking Philip out for the most expensive dinner imaginable, he was left with eight thousand pounds, an absolute fortune for someone from Spitalfields.

At dinner Leon told Philip that he rather fancied himself as a reporter. Not that he'd had much experience—if any—in the field, but he enjoyed writing and he thought it would give him some practice in whatever C. had in mind for his Bosnian assignment. At their dinner in Singapore, C. had mentioned that Leon's cover in getting close to Colonel Dragutin Dimitrijević, the leader of the fascist Black Hand movement, would be that of a reporter for a conservative newspaper.

"What a jolly good idea," Philip had said. "I can see you as some type of society columnist writing about the bedroom scandals of London's elite. I'm going to introduce you to my friend Lord Northcliffe. He's got dozens of rags that he's always trying to offload."

Sure enough, Lord Northcliffe sold Leon a majority share in one of his quite prestigious but lesser-known local newspapers called *The Mayfair Monocle.* Leon began to write a society column under the guidance of a tough-as-nails editor who didn't care that Leon was technically his boss. The column was based on Leon's observations of society figures aided and abetted by Philip, who thought the whole thing a grand lark. His penname was Lady Daphne DeMille, and his first column, which was published two months later, was declared excellent. At least by his mother.

Philip had taken his seat in Parliament, and his Park Lane mansion became the meeting place for an eccentric group of people. They ranged from George Cholmondeley, Earl of

Rocksavage (who was engaged to Philip's sister Sybil), to the artist Rex Whistler and even Winston Churchill on occasion. Philip had little time to spare, but he and Leon became firm friends and spent as much time as they could together. It took Leon a while to feel comfortable in the company of Philip's friends and acquaintances, but Philip helped him work his way through the complexities of high society. There were a few glitches and faux pas, but eventually Leon managed to maneuver his way around questions of his background and focus instead on his life in South and East Africa and Sarawak.

At one point Leon's father took him aside, saying he had a delicate question for his son. "You do know that Philip is a homosexual?"

"Yes," replied Leon, "and he knows that I am not. And the fact that he is doesn't affect our friendship in the least. He is one of the nicest, kindest, and smartest people I know."

"Good," said his father. "I'm pleased you feel that way. My only reason for even bringing it up is that people are prejudiced."

"Too bad for them," said Leon. "They're missing out on a whole group of friends."

It wasn't that Leon was lacking in female companionship. Unbeknownst to his parents, he'd been seeing one of the pub waitresses after hours, and his friendship with Philip brought him into contact with a group of upper-class women who, while disdainful of his breeding at first, declared his skill between the sheets to be the *ne plus ultra*. What Leon had learned at the Heavenly Abode of the Crimson Lotus soon earned him a reputation that was the envy of the most eligible bachelors in London.

For Leon it was a time of happiness. He was a young man enjoying everything normally denied to someone of his status in the hierarchy of society and religion. If there was any guilt that should have attached itself to his ambiguousness, Leon never felt it. The thrill of his prior life as an assassin rapidly gave way to exhilaration of his current excessive lifestyle.

But that all changed on January 11th of 1913.

Chapter 3 – 1913, London

An excellent pie ruined by an indecent proposal

On January 6th of 1913, the First Balkan War still raged. Admiral Pavlos Kountouriotis and the Greek navy defeated the Ottomans and drove them back to the Dardanelles. Things were not going well for the Ottomans, and they continued to deteriorate until the Treaty of London was signed in May of that year. Five days later, just as Leon finished his next column for *The Mayfair Monocle*, he received an invitation from Captain Vernon Kell, head of the domestic division of the Secret Service Bureau, or MI5 as it was soon to be known.

Captain Vernon Kell requests your attendance for lunch at 1pm this Tuesday at Rules restaurant in Covent Garden.

Leon showed the invitation to Abraham, who nodded his head as if he'd been expecting Leon to get it. "Yes, William Melville mentioned you'd be hearing from K., as he now calls himself. Why everyone has to be called by the first letter of their last name beats me. Your boss Cumming is C., Kell is K., and Melville is M. C. is supposedly working with K., but I get the impression that

K. is the big cheese. Though C. would never admit it."

"I don't know about this," Leon said, folding the invitation and slipping it into his jacket. "I honestly don't know if I want to get involved in anything else to do with that clandestine group. I've fulfilled my obligations, and now I'd really like to focus on my column and making *The Monocle* a success."

"Think carefully, *boychik*. You may not have much of a choice."

"Don't bring up the whole curse business. Mama said that wasn't true."

"She did, but I didn't. Of course, she may be right, but is it worth taking a chance? What happens if she's wrong and the curse exists?"

"You're giving me the Pascal 'wager' argument, and I don't buy it."

"From Pascal and his wager, I don't know."

"Pascal said you should believe in God. If He exists, you're in good shape. If He doesn't, you've lost nothing."

"Aha...that's a good argument, and yes, that's what I mean."

"Dad, there's a slight difference. Believing in God or not believing isn't going to get you killed these days. Believing in the curse of the Levites is very likely to get me killed."

"Don't be so sure. You've proved yourself to be a master assassin already. You're good at it."

"That's as maybe, but it isn't something I want to continue doing. I took to it at the start, but now I've had time to think about things, I really want to be a journalist. The sooner I get the *sica* back to Joe in Walvis Bay, the better."

"There's another reason you should see him. Most people I know believe that war is just around the corner. Melville and Kell have been secretly rounding up German spies who they know are passing back vital information to the Kaiser's intelligence service. If the war comes, Britain will begin requiring young men to go to die in Europe. Your friend Philip and his blue-blood associates will all get jobs at home in some form of government service. Unfortunately, that's not how it works for the common man. No, my boy. You won't be that lucky."

"There's no likelihood of conscription in Britain."

"Maybe not, but young men your age will be volunteering by the thousands, and you'll feel terrible if you don't join them."

"When the time comes," Leon said, putting on an air that fell just shy of being righteous, "I hope I'll do what's right."

Abraham gave his youngest son a pat on the shoulder. "I'm sure you will. In the meantime, just see Kell. At the very least the lunch will be good. You know, Rules is the oldest restaurant in London, but the food is fresh." He laughed at his little joke and even Leon cracked a smile.

Leon walked into Rules at ten minutes to one. He wore his best suit, left over from the clothes supplied to him by the agent known only as Leviticus for his first-class voyage on the SS *Gwalior* from Cape Town to Mombasa. It was a beautiful, sunny morning, and he'd bought a pink carnation from a nearby flower seller which he'd placed in his lapel.

Captain Kell, the maître d' informed him, had not yet arrived, but Leon was welcome to sit at the table and peruse the menu while he waited. The table was at the back, set in a corner beneath a painting of The Duke of Wellington. The tables on each side of the one where he sat were unoccupied, though the restaurant was packed with older men in dark suits eating slices of beef with Yorkshire pudding and swilling glasses of claret. He assumed the head of the domestic branch of the Secret Service Bureau had arranged it that way.

None of the other diners had a boutonnière, and Leon wondered if it made him look too conspicuous. For a moment he considered removing his carnation and dropping it under the table but then pushed his concern to the back of his mind. It made him feel good. And why shouldn't he? War might be imminent, but at this moment, peace still reigned supreme. He looked at the menu, which appeared to be focused on dishes designed to leave you sleepy and bloated, and began to consider just what it was that Kell would ask of him. He didn't have long to wait. At precisely one o'clock, a tall man with neatly combed dark hair, an immaculately groomed small mustache, and piercing eyes behind thin pince-nez took the seat to Leon's right.

"I'm Captain Vernon Kell," he said. "And you are Leon Harries?" His accent was posh but by no means condescending.

"Yes, sir," Leon replied, already fully aware that while Cummings had been avuncular, Kell appeared to be all business.

"You may call me K. from now on," Kell said, picking up

a menu, looking at it for no more than a few seconds, and then putting it down as if he'd already memorized the entire thing. "Let's order and then get down to the task at hand. I am meeting with Churchill at two thirty."

"Winston Churchill?" asked Leon.

"Of course, Winston Churchill. How many Lords of the Admiralty named Churchill do you know?"

"I met him at a dinner not long ago."

"I know. I know a great deal about you and your social circle with Sir Philip Sassoon. I also know the services you have provided to Mansfield Cumming and those of your father and brother for William Melville. I don't wish you to take this as flattery, but they all speak extremely highly of your abilities."

"It's good to hear that, but they are abilities I no longer wish to employ."

K. waved away Leon's protest and followed up with a loud *pshaw*. "Cumming said you are prone to bouts of brashness and irresponsibility, which he put down to your immaturity. You should know upfront that I will not tolerate that. Immaturity is no excuse for insubordination. Now, let's order." He nodded his head at a waiter who hovered nearby. "I shall have the chicken, leek and mushroom pie...and for you?"

"I'll have the same," said Leon, who hadn't really thought about what he wanted to eat.

"Excellent," said Kell. "I don't drink at lunch, but if you'd care to partake in something, that's fine."

"No," said Leon, "I have to write my column this afternoon."

"No? Then bring us some of your ginger tea," he said to

the waiter, who scurried off. "I suffer from asthma, and I find that it helps my chest. But to the business at hand. I assume you know about my department from Cumming and through Melville via your father?"

"I know very little," Leon replied. "What I do know is that you and C. split the department. He is responsible for foreign issues while you head the home section."

"Correct. My job of late is to identify and root out subversives."

"What sort of subversives?" Leon asked. He already knew the answer from his father, but he wanted to bait Kell. He didn't like the spymaster's arrogant manner or being talked to as though he already worked for the man.

Kell gave an exasperated grunt. "I would have thought the answer was obvious. We are on the brink of war, Harries. I have an extensive index of foreign agents, mostly German, who are working for the Hohenzollern Court in Berlin to discover just how prepared we are when Germany decides to invade. I have already made numerous arrests, but there are German intelligence agents at work all over the United Kingdom whom I have yet to discover."

"I had no idea."

"Good. If you had I'd be worried that I have a leak in my department."

Their food arrived at that moment, and Kell tucked into his pie as if he hadn't eaten for days. Leon took a small bite and found it quite delectable. "This is delicious," he said. "I've never had chicken, leak, and mushroom pie."

"It may be," replied Kell coldly, "but we are not here to

discuss your prior experience with pies. I have a job which I believe is perfectly suited to you."

"I thought I was working for C.?"

"You are, but he doesn't need your talents at this precise moment. I do." Kell looked at him over his pince-nez as if Leon were something unusual he'd discovered in the pie. "Do you doubt me, sir?"

"No, absolutely not but—"

Kell cut him off. "But nothing. There is a job you need to do that no member of either my department or C.'s can undertake. It is vital, I assure you, to the future safety of England. So any objection you may have will be looked at as a dereliction of your patriotic duty."

Leon put down his knife and fork. He'd suddenly lost his appetite for what only minutes ago had been the best-tasting pie he'd ever eaten. He looked up at Kell and saw someone who wouldn't take no for an answer. "Very well," Leon said, "you'd better tell me about it."

"Stout man. I had a feeling I could count on you," K. said, softening his tone slightly. He looked around to see if anyone nearby could possibly be listening. Then satisfied there wasn't, he leaned forward till Leon could see pieces of pie stuck between his teeth. "You, Harries, are in a unique position. This I am assured of by your friend Philip Sassoon and several *grandes dames* to whose beds I'm told you are a frequent visitor. No, sir, do not blush or begin to protest. It is my job to know all about the people I do business with."

Leon was incensed. "I know you said you won't tolerate brashness, but that is pretty damn low. Spying on a fellow when he's at work in a lady's boudoir. That's intolerable and I won't put up with it."

"Don't *intolerable* and *boudoir* me, my boy. You're a damn roué and there's no getting away from it. And yes, you'll put up with everything I say."

Leon wiped his mouth with his napkin and began to stand. But Kell slapped his hand down on the table, drawing the attention of one or two other diners. "Sit down and calm down. I am not judging you. In fact, your sexual allure is one of the things that makes you attractive from a work standpoint. Though, what those women see in you is beyond me. No, I need both your skills, so listen up."

"Fine," Leon said. "But refrain from the insults if you would. I don't appreciate them." In truth he rather liked the idea that the techniques he'd learned in the Heavenly Abode of the Crimson Lotus had earned him a reputation in London. Secretly he harbored the thought that one day he'd return to Singapore and make love to Lily Tan, and hopefully get higher than a "satisfactory" grade.

"Now," Kell continued, "what do you know about our royalty's ties with Germany?"

"Not more than anyone else, I imagine. I know our king's grandfather was Price Albert of Saxe-Coburg. His wife is a German princess, and one of Victoria's other grandsons is the German Kaiser. Even the Tsar's a cousin if I'm not mistaken."

"You're not. Europe's positively littered with Queen Victoria's offspring, and most of them are randier than you by the way." Kell almost smiled but caught himself. "A joke, not an insult. The German connection is troubling because the last thing we need is more of our aristocracy siding with their Germans relatives. Of course, the Hohenzollerans encourage it, and as they rattle their sabers preparing to fight, they'll use whatever means they have to gain information and sympathy to their cause."

"You're not asking me to assassinate one of the royals, are you?"

"Good God, no. Don't be absurd. We'd never take down an actual member of the Royal Family. No, what I need you to do is get close to Lady Clara FitzHatton and find out just what her husband, George, is passing on to Clara's relatives in Germany."

"You'll need to give me a little more information. I don't know who those people are or what they could be passing on."

"Hmm, hmm," went Kell, putting his hand up to his mouth and patting his moustache as he contemplated just what to tell Leon. He took off his pince-nez and polished them with his napkin. Then apparently satisfied with his thoughts, he continued. "Very well, I suppose you'll need to know more than I intended to divulge at the onset of our lunch."

Leon raised his eyebrows and made a concerted effort not to sound insolent. "I don't profess to understand your job, K. But I do know mine, and it requires enough information for me to, at the very least, have some idea as to who my intended mark is. That is all. More than that is unnecessary and distracting."

Kell nodded. "Good, focus is the key to this business, I find. Here's what you need to know. Lord George FitzHatton has a substantial position in the mobilization division of the admiralty. He is a nincompoop at best and a traitor at worst, and only has the job because of family connections going back to his grandfather's time. His wife, Clara, is the youngest daughter of the Grand Duke of Schleswig-Holstein, and her sister Augusta is married to none other than Kaiser Wilhelm himself. We believe Lord George is passing vital information on to his wife, who in turn feeds it to her brother-in-law's intelligence division."

"Surely Churchill as First Lord of the Admiralty can get rid of him."

"Technically he could and most definitely he should, but without proof we'd have an international incident on our hands. Apart from a highly convoluted family relationship with our own king—no one seems able to work that one out—can you imagine the headline in The London Times: 'Crown accuses Kaiser's brother-in-law of spying'? No, it wouldn't do. Wouldn't do at all. What I have in mind must be done quietly and with the utmost discretion."

"And what is it you have in mind?"

"I would have thought that was obvious. We need you to get Lady Clara to cough up sufficient details about what Lord George has been telling her and then, if I determine it is dangerous to the Empire, he needs to have a nasty accident. Can you pull this off?"

Leon had absolutely no idea whether he could or even how to go about it. But like many twenty-one-year-olds who haven't yet suffered failure, he was not about to say no. "Yes, I can. But gathering evidence is not what I do. I'll need to be paid extra."

"Jesus Lord! So, it's a money thing, is it? I should have known with you people."

"And just what do you mean by that?" Leon asked, knowing full well what Kell was referring to.

"Oh, you know precisely what I mean," Kell sneered.

"Of course I do. But I imagine for someone like yourself whose families have robbed and plundered half the world, an honest wage is something that doesn't come easily."

For a moment Leon thought Kell was about to have apoplexy. Then to his surprise, Kell laughed. "Smith-Cumming said you'd have a smart answer for everything...and he was right, by Jove. Very well, we will add extra if you can supply the evidence."

"Thank you. Now, I'll want some help to set it up?"

"What help? I told you this has to be discreet."

"I need someone to set the stage. Does Churchill know about this?"

"Before I answer that I must remind you that anything we've discussed is classified under the Official Secrets Act, which you are still operating under."

Leon wondered why Kell had said "remind" rather than "inform." He knew the new Official Secrets Act had come into effect just two years before, and as far as he remembered, C. had never asked him to sign it. He shrugged, which Kell took as an acknowledgement.

"Then the answer is yes, Churchill knows and is fully behind this. My meeting this afternoon is to inform him of your willingness. So now, what do you need?"

"Well, the problem is, as I said, I don't know the FitzHattons from a bar of soap. Perhaps Philip Sassoon knows them and could introduce me. However, if I ask him and whatever happens, happens, he'll suspect my involvement in FitzHatton's death. He's no fool and a good friend. I don't wish to lose him as a friend nor take advantage of that friendship. Unless he is assured that the operation is sanctioned by the highest authorities, I'd rather he wasn't involved."

Kell nodded. "I can understand that could be an issue. But tell me—before I ask for Churchill's assistance—tell me what Philip Sassoon knows about you?"

Leon realized that Kell probably knew of his father's involvement with the previous generations of Sassoons and decided there was no point holding anything back. "He knows through his late father the business my family is in. But we've never discussed it openly, and it only came up once at our first meeting."

"I see," Kell said, wiping a piece of pie crust from his lip. "Very well, let me confer with Churchill and I will get back to you. And by the way, don't wear a pink carnation again. It attracts the wrong sort of attention." With that he stood up, straightened his jacket, and walked out, leaving Leon to pay for the meal.

Chapter 4 – 1913 London

Between the sheets and over the balcony

Leon arrived at 25 Park Lane half an hour before the dinner party was due to commence. He was immediately shown up to Philip Sassoon's study by the butler. Philip was standing at the window when Leon entered, but he turned and greeted him with his enigmatic smile. Leon opened his mouth to say something, but Philip held up his hand. "I know what you are about to say, Leon, but there is no need, I assure you. Winston has filled me in—not on everything, mind you—and I am thrilled to be part of the intrigue."

"Thank you," replied Leon, heaving a sigh of relief. When Kell had told him that Churchill had asked Philip to host a dinner party to which Lord and Lady FitzHatton would be invited, he'd been worried. Kell had assured him, however, that it was Churchill who'd broached the idea of a dinner party with Philip and that Philip was perfectly willing to go along.

"I realize you'd never have asked me personally," Philip said.

"No, I wouldn't take advantage of our friendship like that."

"What you should know, if it makes you feel any better, is that through my parliamentary duties I am already associated with the War Department in some small way. Winston has taken me into his confidence, and while he has not fully briefed me on the outcome of your assignment, knowing you I have a bloody good idea. Now, tell me what I need to do."

"I'm supposed to get close to Lady FitzHatton and persuade her to spill the beans on her husband. So, anything you can do to make that happen will be appreciated."

"Consider it done, old chap," said Philip, raising his left eyebrow. "And from what I know about your abilities with the fairer sex, you shouldn't have the slightest problem taking it from there. You'll have to fill me in one of these days on your secret. Perhaps it would work for me, though not quite in the same way I imagine."

"I'd be more than happy to," Leon said with a mischievous grin. "But I'm afraid it would entail a trip to Singapore."

"Even more mysterious and alluring. Well, we don't have much time before the guests arrive, so let me tell you how I've arranged the seating for dinner. You can make any adjustments you like if you feel it will improve your odds."

"Thanks, but I have every faith you've thought this through thoroughly."

"Yes, I dare say I have. Let's see, I shall be at the head of the table with Lady FitzHatton to my right. You will be next to her with my sister Sybil to your right. Her intended, the Earl of Rocksavage, is away, so to keep the gender count equal, I've invited Thomas Lawrence, who is an archaeologist for the British Museum. He's just back from Carchemish in Syria, and I'm sure he's full of fascinating stories about Arabia...likes to be called 'T.E.' by the way. At the bottom of the table, I've placed Lord FitzHatton. To his right is Venetia Stanley, who is being courted by Edwin Montagu, who will be to her right. He's a radical liberal, friend of our Prime Minister Asquith, and besotted with Venetia. Desperate to marry her, but it would mean she'd have to convert to Judaism, and I doubt she will."

"Why on earth did you put her next to him, then?"

"Oh, just for a bit of fun. I have a feeling he'll be so busy trying to impress her that Hatton will be forced to talk to Lawrence, who will bore the pants off him with tales of his archaeological finds and travels. Now, the final couple are the most interesting."

"Do tell."

"You've no doubt heard of George Bernard Shaw?"

"Naturally I've read about him, and you've mentioned that he's visited you before. I've not seen any of his plays, but I've heard enough about him to know how brilliant he is."

"Yes, indeed," Philip replied. "Though between you and me, his wife, Charlotte, is even more intriguing. She's his equal in terms of wit and a rampant socialist to boot. Surprisingly she and Lawrence correspond, though I'm not sure Bernard—as George insists on being called— knows about it. There's nothing sexual about her relationship with Lawrence, who is more in my camp, and rumor has it there's nothing sexual about her marriage with Shaw, either."

"You're an incorrigible font of scandalous information, Philip. But it all sounds perfect. Don't change a thing."

"It should be. My aim is to make sure that you and Clara FitzHatton can have your little tête-à-tête at the dinner table. I shall occupy Shaw, and Sybil will spend her time with Lawrence and Lord FitzHatton. During cocktails I suggest you avoid Clara to allay any suspicion her husband may develop later when you move in, so to speak. I'd suggest you pounce on her ladyship between the roast duck and the Charlotte Ruse."

Just as Leon had come to expect of his friend, things went precisely as Philip had planned. Lawrence and Charlotte conversed quietly while sipping cocktails. Montagu and Venetia talked to Sybil, though their furtive glances suggested that they'd have preferred to be alone. The FitzHattons wanted to see Philip's art, and so he took them on a tour of his house. Leon spoke at length to Shaw, who was fascinated by Leon's meeting with Proust, whom he admired greatly.

"But it is Rajah Charles Brooke that I am most interested in," said Shaw, who was drinking water rather than the glasses of vodka with small pieces of toast and caviar that a footman carried on a large silver tray. "I had dinner with him once when he was here in London after he'd sent me a note telling me how much he admired one of my plays."

"He's a very erudite man," Leon said, but Shaw carried on as if he didn't care to be interrupted.

"You know, some critic once described me as having a morbid dislike of my fellow creatures, which is true by the way. Rajah Charles was an exception. A kindly and compassionate man with what I like to call a healthy rebellious nature. Sassoon tells me you saved his life on a number of occasions?" Once again not waiting for Leon to reply. "Well, you don't much resemble a bodyguard as I envision one to look. And now you are in newspapers. Writing a gossip column of all things. You sound like a character for a play I have yet to write."

"I'm honored," Leon said, trying his best not to smile.

"Don't be," Shaw replied, dropping the left-hand corner of his lip and raising his bushy eyebrow. "You strike me more as the villain than the hero." And with that ringing in Leon's ears, Shaw went over to join his wife and Lawrence. For a minute Leon considered planting a kick on Shaw's retreating backside, but his deliberation was interrupted by Philips's announcement that dinner was ready.

Dinner was not the raucous affair that some of Philip's get-togethers usually were. After some initial banter between Sybil and Philip and a few witty remarks by Charlotte on the state of women's rights directed at Lord FitzHatton (who shrugged them off with a scowl), the conversation retreated—just as Philip had planned—to quiet exchanges with neighboring diners.

"So," said Lady Clara after Phillip had introduced her to Leon, "you are the famous Leon Harries that some of my acquaintances have mentioned." Her voice was low and sultry, and her German accent still angular and direct.

"I'm flattered," he said, trying his best to look imperturbable. "Hopefully they spoke of me in an agreeable manner."

"Oh, they were in agreement, but it had more to do with your abilities than your manner."

"My gosh," said Leon, starting to worry that perhaps his reputation wasn't quite what he'd suspected it was. "Nothing bad?"

"Oh, but it was," said Clara FitzHatton. "Very bad. Apparently, you are an extremely bad boy...." She licked her lips and suddenly Leon felt her hand on his thigh. He looked around to see if anyone was taking notice, but the others were engaged in their respective conversations. Only Philip caught his eye and gave him a half wink.

"I'm sure your friends were exaggerating?" He squirmed as her hand found his crotch.

"Ah," she said as she felt his member begin to respond. "I very much doubt it. No, both Lady Campbell and the Dowager Countess Hamilton were most specific as to your abilities. But then again, they are very English. No, I am convinced that you are indeed a bad boy who needs the attention of a strict German woman. I shall make the arrangements." And with that she turned to Philip and Shaw, leaving Leon blinking like an owl.

My God, he thought. *Success already and we haven't even finished the vichyssoise.* The only thing that had him slightly worried was the "strict German" reference, but he put that down to her upbringing.

After dinner when the men had retired to the smoking room for brandy and cigars, Philip nudged him. "All in order, I trust?"

"I think so," replied Leon, taking a large swig of his brandy. "Though between you and me, I find her quite intimidating."

"And so you should, old chap," Philip replied "The German upper classes have a reputation for rough play. The men slash each other's faces with sabers because they think the scar makes them look more manly. God knows what the women get up to. You've read Krafft-Ebing, haven't you?"

"No, never heard of him."

"Well, you may want to take a gander at his book *Psychopathia Sexualis* before your first encounter with Lady Clara. And if she's wearing spurs and carrying a horse whip, my advice is to run for cover."

"Oh, Jesus," moaned Leon. "You're serious, aren't you?"

"Only half, but for heaven's sake, don't look so glum. I'm sure you can handle a *Prinzessin* who's champing at the bit for a good gallop."

When Leon met Lady Clara FitzHatton—sister of the German empress, daughter of Frederick VIII, Duke of Schleswig-Holstein-Sondergurg-Augusteburg—at 4:30 p.m. in room 118 at the Cadogan Hotel as she d specified in her note, he wasn't sure whether to leap or the bed or make a hasty exit. She was naked, or would have been, were it not for a black bodice and net stockings held up by a garter belt.

"Do you know," she said, slamming the door behind Leon and locking it, "that this is the very room Oscar Wilde was arrested in for acts of gross indecency with his lover, Lord Alfred Douglas?"

"No, no...I didn't," said Leon, trying desperately to slow his breathing.

"Oh, ja," replied Lady Clara, grabbing his belt buckle. "But his acts of indecency are going to be as nothing compared to ours. Now remove your clothes *du sohn einer hundin* and put your *glatte venusmuschel* to work like the bad boy you are."[5]

When at last Clara unhinged herself from Leon and rolled over onto her side of the bed, she let out a deep sigh of satisfaction. "Well, it seems my friends' opinions of your abilities were not exaggerated. I wish my husband could satisfy me in such a manner. But, alas, his performance in the vicinity of my nether regions is sadly lacking. Still, I mustn't complain; he gives me other essentials."

Leon let out a low moan. While Clara had not resorted to any extraneous equipment, the strength in her thighs—no doubt from riding spirited horses—and the sharpness of her nails had left him both exhausted and in a certain amount of pain.

"What was that, *mein liebhaber?*"

"I was just wondering what other essentials he gives you?"

---

[5] *Editorial note: Readers of The Bodyguard of Sarawak, the first installment of Leon's adventures, will recall that the descriptions of his sexual encounters, while quite descriptive in the set-up, are sadly lacking in detail of the act itself. Nevertheless, we can deduce from his description of Clara's accoutrements and Philip Sassoon's reference to Baron von Krafft-Ebing that what transpired was unlike anything Leon had yet encountered in the bedroom. Fortunately, as later events will show, it was new for Clara as well.*

"Ah," she said, giving his nipple a rather painful tweak, "wouldn't you like to know?"

"Yeow...and yes. He clearly doesn't give you satisfaction in your lower extremes, as you say. But I am in no position to give you priceless gifts."

She snorted. "I am a princess; I have no need of gifts."

"Please accept my apologies. I merely meant to find out what it is I could give you that would allow me to compete with your husband."

"Accepted. From you all I desire is a repeat of what you've just done. With perhaps a few variations. My husband, on the other hand, is a weak, weak man. He enjoys being punished by me and in turn provides information which, between you and me, is the only reason I am still with him. But I have said too much."

"What kind of information?" asked Leon, girding his loins in preparation for another bout.

"That's not your concern," she said sharply.

"Yes, indeed," Leon said. "Anything that satisfies you is my concern."

"Then you'll just have to fuck it out of me," she replied as she straddled him for round two.

Half an hour later, Leon had what he needed.

At lunch the next day, Leon provided Kell with the information he had tasked Leon to get.

"I'm uncertain what she meant, but she yelled out something about a Dreyer Memorandum...that was just before she fainted."

"My God," said Kell, almost choking on a piece of roast

beef at both the mention of "fainting" and the memorandum. "If she's passed on the contents of the Dreyer Memorandum, then we are in trouble. How the hell did you get that out of her? Wait a minute," he said, curling his lip. "You didn't torture her, did you?"

"She was screaming, all right. But it wasn't in pain, I assure you."

For a moment Kell stared at him through his pince-nez. Then he let out a disgusted snort. "I see. Well, clearly this cannot continue. I shall fill Churchill in immediately and then give you the go-ahead to terminate Lord FitzHatton. Now, you are to forget you ever heard of the Dreyer Memorandum. Am I clear?"

"Always," Leon said, wiping his mouth with his napkin. "Hang on a second...where are you going? I believe it's your turn to pay." But Kell had already bolted for the door.[6]

The next night during the second act of the British premier of *Der Rosenkavalier* conducted by Thomas Beecham at the Royal Opera House, just when the young lovers belted out their rapturous duet, "*Mitt Ihren Augen voll Tränen*," a young man, his formal suit covered by a long black cape, slipped into one of the boxes. Seconds later, the male occupant of the box made a sound like a deflating Zeppelin, stood up awkwardly, and toppled over the balcony, narrowly missing the stage and

---

[6] *Editorial note: I have searched everywhere I could imagine but so far have found no reference to the Dreyer Memorandum. I can only assume it refers to a report written by Admiral Sir Charles Dreyer, who'd come up with a gunnery fire control system, a form of mechanical computer that was used to calculate firing patterns for warships.*

impaling himself on the oboist's music stand.

"Good grief," whispered one member of the audience. "I know the bloody thing's boring as all hell, but the damn fellow could have waited till intermission."

The papers reported the death of Lord FitzHatton as an accident following a sudden stroke. The coroner, on instructions from someone at Whitehall, failed to mention in his report that FitzHatton's hepatic artery had been severed prior to his unfortunate tumble. No one had seen the mysterious figure who'd slipped into the FitzHatton box a few seconds before and vanished silently into the crowds streaming out of the theater just minutes later.

It was the first and only assignment that Leon received from Kell, whose fee—despite the meager addition for supplying the evidence—was half that of the one paid by C.'s department.

"I should have known the man was a penny-pinching bastard when he stiffed me at lunch," Leon told Abraham.

"It's a good lesson for the future," replied his father as he stacked freshly washed glasses behind the bar. "Always negotiate up front. Remember, ask for twice as much and settle for half that amount. That way they think they're getting a bargain and we get the proper fee."

Chapter 5 - 1913 London

Can the sica cut the Gordian knot of complexity?

At 8 a.m. a telegram from C. arrived at Leon's small apartment in Kensington—he'd moved out of Bessie's bedroom in the pub a few months before. He'd just finished his column for *The Mayfair Monocle* and needed to turn it in by eleven thirty that morning. The London Season was in full swing, and many of the landed gentry had relocated to their London mansions from their country estates to attend the races, cricket matches, balls, and court presentations of their debutante daughters. Leon, through Philip Sassoon, had attended many of the balls, parties, and regattas, and consequently never lacked for gossip for his now highly anticipated columns. He was thoroughly enjoying writing, though he often wondered if a racy society column was where his future lay.

After the FitzHatton affair, he'd decided that his dalliance with the upper echelons of what Philip referred to as the "gentler sex" (and which Leon knew was a far-from-accurate nomenclature for the frustrated female members of the upper classes) had to end. The discreet invitations hadn't stopped, but Leon was beginning to feel more and more like a gigolo, though he'd never even taken a gift for his performances. He was still seeing one of the waitresses from the Sir Sydney Smith, but in truth he was bored and thinking of setting off once more for Africa with the intention of writing an adventure novel. The telegram from C. arrived, so to speak, in the nick of time.

Meet me at The Oriental Club on Hanover Square at one o'clock today. Do not be late. C.

Bloody hell, thought Leon. *Don't these buggers give a damn about my time?* He knew, of course, that they didn't, and it wasn't as though he had anything else to do at that moment. Other than an invitation to have tea with Isadora Duncan that he regretfully declined, this was the most intriguing request he'd had in months. It had been over a year since he'd breakfasted with C. in Singapore, and he had all but given up ever hearing from him again.

Leon dropped off his column at *The Monocle*'s office on Lombard Lane just off Fleet Street at precisely eleven thirty. The editor gave him a grunt, which meant he liked it. He'd yet to actually say he liked Leon's writing, but their communication had progressed from a disgruntled moan to a dismissive grunt. Leon chatted briefly with a couple of his fellow reporters and decided to walk to the Oriental Club, making a diversion to Jermyn Street for a solitary and rather early lunch at Wiltons Restaurant.

He arrived at The Oriental Club two minutes to one and was shown up to the Smoking Room by a steward. C.

was sitting in one of the blue leather armchairs smoking a cigar and chatting to a large man with a neatly trimmed beard and a military bearing. C. signaled Leon to wait a moment. The large man gave a guffaw at something C. said and then walked off to chat with someone else, who was enveloped in a cloud of pipe smoke.

"Ah," said C. after Leon had sat down in the chair next to him. "You have a distinct oystery odor about you."

"I stopped at Wiltons on the way for two dozen Jersey Rock oysters."

"Can't look at the blasted things without wanting to throw up," C. said. "Had a rotten one a couple of years ago and it played merry hell with my innards. But oysters ain't what I wanted to discuss. The time has come when we need to put into play the discussion we had in Singapore."

"Ah yes, I thought that's what you'd want to talk about. I read the Balkan combatants were about to sign a peace treaty."

"That is indeed so. The Treaty of London is to be signed in less than a week. Though God knows how it'll play out. I wouldn't be surprised if five minutes after the ink has dried, the damn Bulgarians launch an attack on their former allies. Must be something in the water in that part of the world. Everyone's looking to cause mischief on a grand scale. They can't help themselves. In my opinion, the swarthier the population, the more belligerent they are. And I include the women. Here, before we begin, try some of that snuff. Does marvelous things to the old sinuses." He pointed to an old ram's head, which together with spoons and snuff rakes held pride of place on a sideboard. "It'll help with the briny smell."

"I'll give it a miss for the moment," Leon said, eyeing the grotesque object. "But I take it that means Colonel Dragutin Dimitrijević is now back to his old tricks."

"Without doubt. He and the Black Hand—or 'Union or Death' as the blighters call themselves—have already made one attempt on the life of the Austro-Hungarian emperor, Franz Joseph. That plan was thwarted, fortunately, but we have reason to believe they're planning another at some point. Either on his life or the heir-presumptive, his nephew the Archduke Franz Ferdinand." He shook his head and blew out a smoke ring. "Can't these nobs think of first names other than Franz? It gets awfully confusing. Anyway, from what we can make out, they're recruiting some thoroughly dangerous individuals from another group called the Young Bosnians to help their cause. If these swine succeed, and I fear they might very well do so, then all hell will break loose. The Germans will jump in. The Russians will pile in on top of them. However, at the moment—"

"But," interrupted Leon, already slightly confused and desperate to stop C. before he confused him even more, "I thought we and the Germans were getting on rather well at present. I just read an article about how there's to be a joint review of British and German fleets at Kiel in the near future...to celebrate our wonderful relations."

"Yes, yes," said C. dismissively. "That's what you newspaper chappies are keen to report, isn't it? No one wants to think of a war...we're too civilized...too joined at the hip globally. And it is true: The considered opinion of some politicians—and it is an ill-conceived opinion, I believe—is that there will be no war with Germany."

"Well, that's a relief."

"No, it's not. They're blasted idiots, the lot of them."

"But I assume you still need me to take care of Colonel Dragutin Dimitrijević?"

"No, and if you'd let me finish without constant interruptions, I'd appreciate it. What I was about to say is that I need you to take care of Colonel Alfred Redl."

Leon had become used to C. making no sense. He shook his head. "Who did you say?"

"Do pay attention, sir. We have precious little time. I said I need you to assassinate Colonel Alfred Redl?"

"I have no idea who he is other than Redl sounds like a German name."

"Galician, actually. Part of the Austrian Empire. And I'd be surprised if you did know who he was; the man's a spy. Look, the whole situation is incredibly complicated with more moving parts than Big Ben."

"I don't know how many that is."

"Neither do I, dammit. I'm using an analogy. Or is it a metaphor?"

Leon shrugged. "I always get mixed up myself."

C. gave an impatient snort. "Will you kindly shut the hell up and just listen? What I am attempting to convey is that we are in a predicament buried deep in the bowels of an enigma. And that predicament is as rampant in the rest of the world as it is here. Everyone suspects that there may be a war. Most people don't want it to happen. Some people think it cannot be prevented. A few think it can. There are generals advising emperors to make preemptive strikes before the other side is prepared. There are those clamoring for détente."

"I'm afraid I have no idea what you just said. There is going to be a war...there isn't going to be a war. Which is it?"

"Good lord. Education has gone downhill since my time at school. What I'm saying, and you'd better get it through your thick noggin, is that we are sitting blissfully confused atop a mountain of kindling. All it will take to set the world ablaze is one match. Our job is to prevent that match from striking. The match that is Dimitrijević must wait. Right at this moment, the match we must douse is Colonel Alfred Redl."

"You sound a little less sure of what you called 'the inevitable' than you did in Singapore...and I say that with the greatest respect, C."

"Everything you say hovers somewhere between insolence and ignorance, but your observation this time is correct. I am torn between what I believed last year and what I see today. Nonetheless my fear remains and I need to alleviate at least part of that in the next week by removing Colonel Redl before the Austrians arrest him and discover that he works for us rather than the Russians as they currently suspect."

"I see," said Leon, not really seeing anything at all. "But I need to understand a little more if I am to have any chance of success."

"More will not necessarily be beneficial, I fear. The critical thing is that it's a jumble of information and misinformation. And the more of it that comes available, the more complicated the situation gets. If I give you too much—and you were the one who told me this in Mombasa—you will lose focus. So, I will try to make it as clear as I can by telling you as little as I must for you to complete the task."

Once again C., in his attempt at clarification, failed. He took a huge pinch of snuff, sneezed once, and then blew what looked like a small brown creature into his handkerchief. "At this very moment, alliances between the empires are held together by string and beeswax. As you'll no doubt recall from your Kenya and Sarawak experiences, many military leaders and members of the aristocracy are doing their best to shift those alliances. The Kaiser and his cousin the Tsar are exchanging friendly letters. Germany is staying out of it, but they are attached by the old umbilical to Austro-Hungary. The Russians hate the Austrians with a passion. The Germans can't stand the French who, despite history, are allied with us and the Russians. Though, of course, the Russians think the French are a bunch of socialists and the French in turn see the Russians as the oppressors of the people. We have the same ties through our royal family connections to both Germany and Russia, but of course we are signatories to the Triple Entente with France and Russia. Now I could get into the whole colonial issue and the race to split up Africa, but for now I'll leave that alone."

"So, back to Colonel Redl," said Leon, wondering what C. had left out that could possibly have added more confusion to his already convoluted explanation.

"Colonel Alfred Redl, up until last year when he became chief of staff of the VIII Corps under Baron von

Gieslingen, was chief of intelligence for the Austrian Army. He's a brilliant man who set up some of the most impressive counter-intelligence operations of any I've seen. But he has his weaknesses. Which is how we managed to recruit him about ten years ago. I'll go into his weaknesses if necessary. The brilliant part of what we've done—and this will remain classified on pain of death—is that he believes he is working for the Russians. And as of a few days ago, so do the Austrians."

"So you need him eliminated before the Austrians find out the truth...but how could they if he doesn't know it himself?"

"Oh, they'll find out eventually. His successor, Major Maximillian Ronge, who if anything is far smarter than Redl, will check bank transfers and letters that Redl hasn't bothered to examine closely enough. As careful as our man in Vienna has been, there is always something that is overlooked. Redl's only reason for not being as thorough with his own affairs is because we pay him a fortune, and people driven by avarice and desire for expensive items rarely bother to take as many precautions as those driven by patriotism. But as I said he is no fool, and if he'd been as thorough as someone in his position should be he would have realized that his paymaster is in fact His Majesty's Government."

"Time is of the essence, I imagine."

"Oh yes, indeed. Two days ago, my agent found out that Ronge intercepted two letters sent to Redl containing money. At the moment, Ronge thinks the letters come from Russian agents, which they are designed to do. However, should they take Redl in for interrogation, the ruse will be exposed. My agent is convinced that it's only a matter of days before Ronge will be able to trace them back to him. Needless to say, if we are found to be the spymasters, it will be the most embarrassing state of affairs for Britain. The Russians will be furious, and any trust we've garnered with the Austrians and Germans will vanish like footprints on a beach."

"Well, I suppose I'd better go home to pack."

"No, you're leaving for Vienna in twenty minutes. We have a fast boat standing by to get you to France and then an even faster car that will get you to Paris by five o'clock to catch the Orient Express. If all goes well, you'll be in Vienna late tomorrow morning. You'll have no time to pack, so once again you'll find a portmanteau with sufficient outfits aboard the train."

"And what happens if it doesn't go well?" asked Leon, feeling a sudden apprehension.

"We fail. And if we do, well…God alone knows what happens. So, my point is: don't fail."

"I appreciate your confidence in me, C. But I am beginning to have my doubts about this sort of work. I'm enjoying my life as a columnist, and I see that as my future. Surely you have an agent available who is more competent?"

"The short answer is, I don't. The long answer—and no, don't roll your eyes at me; I know you think I ramble on at times, but I do so for a purpose. I do so to convey the complexity of the world as it enters this transitionary phase. There are myriad cracks in the foundations of the old empires that make up Europe. All will fall eventually, but it cannot happen all at once. We need people with your skill to ensure the collapse happens in an orderly fashion. If I do not doubt your importance then you should not either. You are the only person who can take out Redl. You have learned diplomacy from your friend Philip Sassoon. You have perfected—or so I heard—certain other techniques learned in Singapore. You have retained the skill that has coursed through the blood of your family for millennia. No, you are perfectly qualified."

Leon shrugged then nodded his head slowly. C. was right. Fate—or whatever force flowed through the universe— had chosen a direction for him, and short of a few bumps and bruises along the way, it had been a pretty good journey so far.

"You'll be met in Vienna by my agent," C. continued. "He will fill you in on details that will get you close to your target. You are Chris Wilmot of *The Daily Mail*, interviewing people who've attained wealth and status the hard way. Just the type of drivel the *Mail* readers lap up. Not sure who the people you'll interview are exactly, but you're a smart fellow; you can work something out. Now," he said, picking up a thick envelope from the table next to him, "here is sufficient funds for the trip. I shall want a full account on your return. Should you need to reach me at any point, send a telegram to this person at this address." He handed Leon a small piece of paper on which was written a name and address that Leon didn't recognize. "I shall get the telegram and respond to you." He retrieved a wallet from the envelope and gave it to Leon. It contained a wad of five-, ten-, and fifty-pound notes.

"Talking of money," said Leon, remembering what his

father had said about asking for half of the fee up front, "I'd like to request—"

C. stood up and grabbed Leon's hand. "Good luck, my boy. I'd happily chat more, but there's a car waiting for you outside."

Chapter 6 - 1913 Aboard the Orient Express and Vienna

In the world of fog and fury, no one is who they say they are

A porter with a hand cart on which rested a well-used leather suitcase met Leon on the Orient Express platform at the Gare de l'Est in Paris.

"We must hurry, Monsieur Wilmot," he said, running up to a door where a conductor, resplendent in a light blue coat with gold buttons and piping, was about to blow his whistle.

"I've been hurrying the whole damn day," Leon said, swinging up onto the train just as the porter handed his suitcase and ticket to the conductor. He was both tired and hungry after vomiting what was left of his oyster lunch half way across the Channel as the Navy launch bounced its way across the swells. His legs felt like jelly and all he wanted to do was clean up, have a drink and dinner, and then sleep for as long as it took the train to reach Vienna.

Leon wasn't aware if there were better—or worse—sleeping compartments on the train. He didn't care; his was splendid. It was obvious that the Compagnie Internationale des Wagons-Lits had spared no expense to transform a lowly train compartment into a luxurious hotel room on rails. The walls were covered in mahogany with highly polished trim and the day bed in brown and teal velvet. It was, he decided, quite the most splendid accommodation he'd had since his suite at the Raffles Hotel in Singapore. Nothing looked out of place or the least bit garish. And yet, amongst the well-ordered and tasteful appearance, there lurked the chill of mystery and danger that crept up his trouser leg until it found his spine.

"When monsieur wishes to sleep," said the steward, who'd shown him his quarters, "please inform me and I will make up the bed. Here you have your wash basin, and the toilette is at the end of the corridor."

Leon had no idea what clothes were in the suitcase, but he hoped there was a suit to replace the now rather rumpled tweed one he'd worn the entire day. "What is the dress for dinner?" he asked the conductor, hoping it wasn't a dinner jacket as he'd still not mastered tying his bow tie.

"You will find many of the men in dinner jackets, monsieur, but a dark evening suit is acceptable. The one you are wearing unfortunately will not do at all. I can, if you like, have it pressed for you by the time we arrive in Vienna, which I believe is your final destination."

Leon thanked him and once the steward had left his compartment opened the suitcase. Clearly who ever had packed it for him had considered the dress requirements; he found a dark suit, white shirts and collars, and an assortment of socks, underwear, and ties. There was also a navy-blue blazer and grey trousers for day wear. He opened the toiletry bag and found a hairbrush, razor, shaving soap, a toothbrush, and a tube of Colgate toothpaste, which he immediately used to cleanse his mouth of regurgitated oysters.

It was six forty-five when Leon made his way to the saloon car for a pre-dinner cocktail. He felt a sense of déjà vu, as if he were back in the first-class lounge on the SS *Gwalior* from Cape Town to Mombasa. Couples, mostly older, were sitting in the leather armchairs smoking cigarettes and drinking champagne, sherry, and martinis. Leon found an empty chair and asked a passing waiter for a martini. He'd had his first one aboard the SS *Gwalior* and had come to appreciate the euphoric kick from the iced gin and vermouth. There were a few single people in the car, mostly men who looked like diplomats, talking quietly amongst themselves. Not that Leon was *au fait* with the physical appearance of diplomats, but these were men with short, neatly brushed hair, well-trimmed pencil mustaches, and condescending looks that spoke of jealously maintained social positions. He imagined they were on their way to their embassies to try to repair relationships—or possibly destroy them. His musings were interrupted by a steward who leaned forward so that his words were discreet.

"Monsieur Wilmot, I understand you will wish to take dinner, but it is my misfortune to tell you that there are no single tables left."

"I don't mind," replied Leon. "I'm just hungry, so if someone doesn't mind sharing, you can tell them I promise only to open my mouth to shovel food in it."

"Very well, monsieur," replied the steward, "please allow me to enquire." Leon watched as the steward moved through the car asking some of the single people whether they'd share. Some of the men didn't even look up as they shook their heads, but one or two glanced in his direction before declining. The steward disappeared into the dining car and emerged a minute or so later to tell Leon that there was a diner who'd just sat down that would be delighted to sup together.

"Excellent," said Leon. "Then if you wouldn't mind transferring my martini to the table, I will join him immediately so that he doesn't have to scoff away on his own."

"It is not a 'he,' monsieur, but a woman travelling alone to Vienna from Paris."

"All the better," replied Leon, giving the steward a wink as he placed his martini on the silver tray. "I'm not averse to dining with someone's granny. Lead on, my good man."

The woman at the table brought back Rajah Charles Brook's admonition about making assumptions before one knew the facts. Leon had imagined an old dowager who'd examine him carefully through her lorgnette before deciding that she'd made a horrible mistake in inviting him to join her. Instead, he found an exotically beautiful woman with blue-black hair and olive skin, and a long, elegant neck that spoke of poise and confidence and on which rested a single strand of pearls. She was older than him by as much as ten years, he thought, but not beyond the bounds of acceptability.

"My thanks for allowing me to join you," Leon said as he sat down.

"Oh," she replied with a wave of her hand, "you are welcome. Most of the people on this train wouldn't be caught dead sitting with me." She spoke English with an accent that reminded Leon a little of a visitor from Dutch Batavia he'd met at one of the Rajah's dinner parties in Sarawak.

"I hope I'm not being presumptuous," Leon said, knowing full well that he was, "but I find it hard to believe that any man in his right mind would not wish to sit with you."

"You are most sweet to say that, but then again you have no idea who I am."

"Well," Leon replied, taking a sip of his martini which the steward had set down together with an elaborate menu, "as we are dinner companions, perhaps you would tell me."

"Perhaps I will," she said, picking up the menu. "But I think we should order first." Leon tried to read her eyes, but they were so dark and deep that he could discern nothing of what she thought.

They started with caviar and blinis, chopped shallots, and hard-boiled eggs served with small glasses of chilled vodka. Leon was thrilled to see his mysterious host bolt the vodka back as if it were something she did both frequently and with abandon. She treated the Pouilly-

Fuissè with equal recklessness, and it was only after her first sip of Château Beychevelle during the Charolais roast beef fillet and rosemary potatoes that she began to tell Leon who she was.

"On stage I am known as Mata Hari, but my real name is Margaretha Zellie. MacLeod was my married name."

"Margaretha sounds Dutch, but MacLeod is Scottish, is it not?"

"Yes, I was born in Leeuwarden in the Netherlands, and my ex-husband—may he rot in hell—had Scottish heritage. We lived for a period of time in Java."

"I thought you had a hint of Batavian in your accent...I was in Sarawak a year or so ago and met someone from there at a dinner party. You sound similar. But why do you call yourself Mata Hari?"

"It means 'sun' in the Malay language, and it suits the exotic style of my routine. I am a dancer, or perhaps I should say I was a dancer. Now so many young women— much younger than me—have usurped me as the premier entertainer in Europe. And all these men with their sexually repressed wives—" she looked around at the other diners

"—show nothing but disdain when once they would line up to tell me how infatuated they were with me."

"I have a hard time believing that, madame. Not how infatuated these old codgers were with you, but how a younger woman could compete with perfection?"

Mata Hari laughed and patted his cheek, causing some old duffer to choke on his claret. "For someone so young, you are quite the charmer. Tell me about yourself."

"Not much to tell," Leon replied. Any fatigue he'd felt

before dinner had vanished the second he'd sat down, which was fortunate because he didn't think he'd be getting much sleep that night. "I'm just a reporter for a London paper on my way to Vienna to interview some of the brass hats."

"Which ones? I know a few brass hats, as you call them. Perhaps, as I find you quite agreeable, I can make an introduction."

"Oh, really?" Leon felt a twinge of panic. The last thing he needed was someone who could tie him to Colonel Redl.

"Yes," said Mata Hari, "I plan to see my old friend Count von Hötzendorf. He is the *Feldmarschall* of the entire Austro-Hungarian army. I would be more than happy to make an introduction."

"You are most kind, but I write for a low-brow newspaper more interested in sensationalism than class. Your friend is far too important to waste his time with anything like that. No, my sights are set a little lower. My contact in Vienna has arranged for me to meet some hussars and dragoons who I'm told live quite interesting lives off the battlefield."

"How boring," said Mata Hari. "But in any case, I don't believe you."

Leon went cold. "You don't?"

"No. Not a soul on this train is who they say they are. Why would you be any different?"

"I jolly well am a reporter for *The Daily Mail*. I can show you my press card." He made to reach for his wallet knowing full well that C. had failed to give him the aforementioned card.

She gave a dismissive snort. "What does a press card prove? Anyone could forge one. No, my young friend, you are far too much of a *beau parleur* to be a reporter."

"Madame," said Leon, trying his best to sound indignant, but failing miserably. "Perhaps your imagination has been seduced by this magical train."

"What do you know?" she asked. "You are but a youth who is blissfully unaware of the goings-on aboard the Orient Express."

"Steady on," Leon hissed, "I'll have you know I've done more things in my twenty-odd years than most men do in their lives. If you're going to throw out wild deductions and accusations...."

Mata Hari laughed. "Life, as you'll discover, is all deductions and accusations. If you are to succeed, you will need to understand that is how the world of fog and fury turns. Deductions...evidence—true or false, it doesn't matter...accusations."

"Well, I don't, and I have no idea what you mean."

"I will give you an example," she said. "Do you see that man over there? The one with the gold pince-nez?" She dabbed her mouth with her napkin and rolled her eyes in the direction of a large man with thin red hair neatly parted in the middle and a face the color of a boiled lobster.

"Yes, what of him?"

"In your opinion," she dropped her voice and leaned forward, "who is he?"

"Oh, I don't know...he looks like some wealthy industrialist. Probably on his way to conclude a deal somewhere or other. But after what you've just told me, he's most likely a spy."

"Excellent," she said. "Based purely on something I said, you have made a deduction. So now you are sufficiently intrigued to look for evidence."

Before Leon could respond, Mata Hari continued. "His name, by the way, is Charles Beauregard. He works for George Ladoux, head of the Deuxième Bureau, and he is on his way to the Kingdom of Bulgaria on a secret mission. There, you see, a simple opinion from one party has been confirmed with facts from another. All that is left is for you to make an accusation to the authorities in Vienna, and he will be arrested and shot."

"And why would I do that?"

"Because that is how you gain power and position."

"I see," said Leon. "But how do I know the so-called facts you have supplied as to Monsieur Beauregard's occupation are indeed facts and once again not just figments of your imagination?"

"You don't, but, as I said, fact or fiction…it doesn't matter. You have heard of the Dreyfuss Affair?"

"Of course, the French army captain accused of spying for the Germans and sent to Devil's Island. What a huge travesty of justice that was. But now he has been fully exonerated."

"Indeed. But his conviction was based on the opinion of an anti-Semitic officer. The 'facts' were concocted by a 'handwriting expert' of dubious qualification, and within days Dreyfuss was accused, arrested, and transported to hell. *J'Accuse* as the great Zola so perfectly put it."

"But why are you telling me all this?"

"Because you are as much a reporter as most of the people aboard this train say they are something else. But don't worry, whatever your secrets, they are safe with me. Now, if you are finished eating your syllabub, perhaps you'd like to come to my carriage for a night cap."[7]

---

[7] *Editorial note: As with all of Leon's intimate liaisons, he is selfishly sparse on the details. However, with Mata Hari he is even more so, leading me to believe that he genuinely liked and respected the woman who was to become the most notorious spy of WW1. (Although recent evidence suggests she was more of a scapegoat than a villain.) Then, of course, perhaps Leon and Mata Hari simply sat and chatted over a brandy. I sincerely hope not.*

Chapter 7 - 1913 Vienna

Leon comes out the closet

To further add to the intrigue of those who Mata Hari said rode the Orient Express, Leon noticed that most of the passengers failed to acknowledge each other as they stepped onto the platform of the Vienna Westbanhof. It was if they were all strangers to each other. He wondered if there'd been other assassins on board, and he hoped if there had, their assignments didn't include Colonel Redl.

He looked around for Mata Hari to ask her if he could see her again. He was about to walk over when she shook her head and he stopped in his tracks. She gave Leon no more than a glance as she directed a porter to take her travelling cases to a large maroon Mercedes Phaeton that was parked alongside the platform. Leon saw a man in the back of the car in a military uniform with enough gold braid to suggest that he was someone of importance.

His musings were interrupted by a short, plump, bearded man in a bowler hat and long grey coat who walked by him, stopped for a moment, and proceeded towards the main part of the station. In those few seconds he'd whispered to Leon to follow him. He walked quickly and Leon, struggling with his heavy suitcase, almost lost sight of him as he made his way through the crowds. The man exited the station's main entrance on the Europaplatz and got into a black carriage. As Leon approached, the driver of the carriage jumped down and grabbed his suitcase. "You must to get in quickly," he said in a thick Slavic accent.

Leon opened the door expecting to see the bowler-hatted man, but the cab was empty. Just as he sat back trying to make sense of what was going on, there was a tap on the window and he looked out to see another carriage that had pulled up right next to his. The door was open and the little man he'd followed beckoned for him to get in.

"Sorry for the deception," he said to Leon in English, though his accent was Russian, "but you never know who's watching these days. Hopefully they didn't see our little switch-over and will follow the other carriage rather than ours."

"I assume you're my contact here?" said Leon.

"Yes, but more than that I can't say. The less you know about me, the better. As it is we have very little time. The mark is currently at the Hotel Klomser—an expensive but discreet establishment—with his lover, Stefan Horinka. He is dining with Generaladvokat Viktor Pollak tonight and will return to the hotel by eleven thirty. At that point you will have no more than thirty minutes to kill him and make your getaway."

"Why only thirty minutes?" Leon asked. The man

looked decidedly nervous, and the whole thing was sounding more and more ludicrous by the minute.

"Because Ronge, Urbański, Vorliček, and the Deputy Chief of the General Staff, Franz von Hoefer, will be arriving shortly after that to arrest Redl."

"Other than Ronge I don't know those names, but I must say you seem awfully well-informed."

"It is my job to be informed."

"I assume so, but how do you know everything to the last detail?"

"That is none of your concern."

"Well then, how do I know it's accurate? I don't know who you are, and you've given me information that's almost too perfect. I have a feeling this is a trap, and I have no intention of falling into it."

"Very well," said the bowler-hatted man, removing his hat and putting it in his lap. "C. warned me that you might be difficult."

"I'd hardly call trying to ensure I'm not going to be thrown into an Austrian prison and possibly shot 'being difficult.'"

"Hmph." The man's hands tensed, and he began to twist the rim of his hat as if he were making a pizza. "You should not be questioning a superior."

"First of all, I'm a freelancer, and second I'd certainly not call you superior without knowing more about you. How are you superior? If it's in rank, then I don't give a fig. I'm strictly pay-by-the-hour."

"You are an impertinent young dog. I shall not reveal my name, but you can rest assured that I have been placed here by C." The man sounded both frustrated and angry.

"You sound Russian."

"I am Russian, but I work for the British. My job has been to ensure that Redl believes he is supplying the information to Russia and to pay him handsomely for that information. The reason I have the details of Redl's movements is because I have someone extremely high up in the *Evidenzbureau* who too is on my payroll. Does that satisfy you sufficiently? Or perhaps I should telegram C. and inform him that you are not up to the job."

"Too late for that given the timing you're proposing. No, sir. I don't have a choice at this stage, but I warn you: This had better not be a trap." Leon tried to sound threatening, but the little man saw right through him.

"You are quite naïve for someone who I'm told is a highly experienced assassin. You should know that in our business, in the world of fog and fury, there are no guarantees. Every footstep may be that of the enemy. Every situation has the potential to be a trap."

The man had used the same phrase—"fog and fury"—as Mata Hari had the previous evening, and Leon wondered if it was some sort of code amongst secret agents. "Unlike you," he said, "I'm not a spy. I don't understand the business, though I do understand the odds of success, and I don't work when they are not in my favor. So now, tell me exactly what the plan is so that I can decide how best to carry out my assignment."

The now bare-headed man stopped fidgeting with his hat. His nostrils flared and his eyes, which Leon thought were beady to begin with, narrowed into slits more commonly encountered when one is face-to-face with a venomous snake. "In a few moments we will drop you a block from the Klomser, where Redl is staying in room one on the second floor. Your bag is there already in a room that has been reserved in the name of Herr Chris Wilmot. Your occupation on the reservation is journalist. A note was sent to Redl asking for an interview which he refused, but if you confront him in the lobby on his return from his dinner, he will at the very least know who you are. It will be your decision to kill him then and there or go with him up to his room."

"And what is my escape plan?"

"There will be a taxi at the rear entrance to the hotel. It will wait for you for no more than thirty minutes after Redl enters the hotel. You will have no time to return to your room after the kill."

"What about my clothes?"

"All your clothes will be removed from the suitcase at some time this evening so that no one can trace your origin from the labels. It was impossible to get Russian-manufactured clothes in the time available. The taxi will take you to a safe house. Tomorrow, we will get you across the border to Munich, where you will be met by another agent."

"But what if it takes more than thirty minutes?"

The little man clicked his tongue. "You are full of 'what ifs.' If you do not complete the assignment in the time allotted, you will run into Ronge and the group coming to arrest Redl. You may get away by showing your press credentials or claiming that you are another of his lovers, but my feeling is you will be arrested and tried as a spy. Now, this is where you get out. Check into your room. Then I suggest you walk around the city for a while and take a late dinner. You will not wish to be sitting in the lobby of the Klomser for too long or you will raise suspicion."

It had been a long afternoon and evening, most of which Leon had spent walking around Vienna. Under normal circumstances he'd no doubt have marveled at the magnificent architecture of the emperor's imperial city, but his head was full of thoughts that spun around like an empty fairground carousel. If indeed it wasn't a trap, and he couldn't work out why it should be—after all, he was on the right side—then it felt very poorly planned on the part of C. and his agents.

A thick mist swirled around the city as Leon made his way back to the hotel after dinner. He'd eaten a decent schnitzel and drunk a glass of Weissgipfler wine at the Lindenkeller Restaurant and tried his best to eavesdrop on his fellow diners to understand what the mood in the city was. But his grasp of the language was poor, not enough to form any opinion of the mood of the people, so he only caught bits and pieces. It was now close to eleven o'clock, and the crowds had thinned to a few stragglers in evening dress looking for taxis to take them home.

Nothing felt right to Leon, but short of bailing before he reached the hotel, he had no idea what to do. In this pensive and pessimistic mood, he shuffled up Bankgasse to the hotel entrance on Herrengasse, desperately trying to form a scenario in his mind that could possibly end in him not getting arrested. His anxiety was almost overwhelming, and he cursed C. for talking him into taking the assignment and himself for even thinking that such a harebrained, ill-conceived plot might work.

The lobby of the Klomser was large and ornate with red-velvet chairs trimmed in gold and dark mahogany tables. When he'd checked in that afternoon, he thought the elaborately lit room anything but the "discreet establishment" Bowler Hat had described in the carriage. Bellmen in scarlet uniforms dashed about, and waiters in starched aprons brought tea and pastries to the important-looking guests sitting reading newspapers or engaged in muffled conversation. But now, at this late hour, the hotel was eerily dark and empty. The huge chandelier had been turned off, and just a few table lamps cast a soft glow over the large room, adding a sense of dread to Leon's already-despondent mood.

A tired-looking receptionist straightened up from the desk over which he'd been slumped. "Ah," he said to Leon, "Herr Wilmot." He reached behind the counter to the key rack and handed Leon the key to room five. Leon saw that the key to room one was still on its hook, which meant Bowler Hat's information was correct and Redl had not yet returned. That made him feel a little better.

"Is it possible to get some coffee here in the lobby?" Leon asked. "I have no desire to go up to my room just yet."

"Of course, Herr Wilmot. Please to take a seat and I will bring it out to you. Forgive me, but it is only me on duty at this hour, so I must do everything myself."

"Oh dear," Leon said, opening his hands. "I don't wish to cause you any unnecessary work."

The receptionist clicked his heels. "Nothing is

unnecessary to ensure our guests' satisfaction. Please, I shall be but a few moments."

Two minutes later he emerged from behind the desk carrying a tray with a cup and a silver pot of steaming coffee, which he set down on the table next to the chair into which Leon had slumped. His mind was still whirring as it contemplated everything that could go wrong.

"Is everything in order, *mean Herr?* You look very weary."

"Thank you," Leon replied. "It has been a busy afternoon and evening, and I am thinking of the story I must write for my newspaper by tomorrow morning."

"Ah yes, I understand you are a journalist," the receptionist said, giving Leon a low bow. "If there is anything that you need? Pen, paper, perhaps the use of a typewriter which we have recently acquired? It will be my pleasure to provide assistance."

Leon thanked him for his offer and then sat contemplating what his move would be the moment Redl entered the hotel. The more he thought about Bowler Hat's idea of him accosting Redl in the lobby, the more ludicrous it seemed. There was no possible way that the receptionist would fail to notice the interaction between the two men, especially if Redl was unnerved at being confronted by a journalist. He'd be forced to report the incident to the authorities when they began to investigate the next morning. No, the most sensible thing he could do was to be out of the reception area when Redl returned.

Leon took a final sip of coffee, wished the receptionist a pleasant night, and then walked up the staircase towards his room. He stopped on the first landing and looked back at the lobby to make sure the receptionist wasn't watching. Satisfied that he wasn't, Leon slipped behind a bushy fern in a large marble urn that occupied one corner of the landing. The spotlight that lit it during the day was turned off, and the shadows, Leon thought, would provide a perfect spot to watch the lobby. He removed his shoes, then withdrew the *sica* from the leather scabbard strapped to his left ankle. He clasped it tightly and found once again—just as he had in Kenya and Sarawak—that the simple act of holding the dagger slowed down his mind, until suddenly the scenario in which he'd kill Redl began to unfold.

The timing could not have been more opportune, for at that moment Redl entered the hotel. He wore a dark coat trimmed with fur and a homburg hat, which he removed as he approached the reception desk. While he seemed older and more bloated than the man C. had described at lunch, there was no mistaking his close-cropped hair, protruding ears, and neatly trimmed mustache.

Leon watched as Redl took his key from the receptionist and walked towards the staircase. Then Redl stopped and turned back to the desk. Their voices were muffled, but Leon understood enough to hear Redl ask the receptionist if anyone had looked for him. Satisfied that no one had, Redl began to slowly climb the stairs. His head was bowed, and he looked to Leon like a man shouldering a heavy burden. Redl failed to see Leon as he passed the urn, nor did he hear his stockinged feet behind him as he walked toward room one. As he unlocked the door and pushed it open, Leon stepped out of the shadow.

"Colonel Redl," whispered Leon, "a moment of your time."

Redl stiffened and slowly turned towards the figure who'd crept up behind him. He looked at Leon not with surprise or shock but rather with acceptance, as if he knew what was about to happen and welcomed it. He opened his mouth to say something, but all that came out was a low moan as the *sica* ripped through his coat into his liver. Redl stiffened for no more than a second or two and then sank to his knees as Leon pulled the dagger sideways, severing his hepatic artery. Leon caught him under his arms before he toppled over and, leaving the *sica* embedded to prevent too much blood from gushing out the wound, he dragged Redl into his room.

It was a large room, and Leon was breathing heavily by the time he'd pulled, tugged, and carried the now-dead Colonel Redl to the four-poster bed. He heaved him up, withdrew the *sica*, and flipped Redl over onto his back so that the blood ran into the mattress. There was no point trying to take off his clothes nor pull the thick duvet over the body. Such tactics wouldn't fool anyone for more than a second. The pungent smell of blood, urine, and feces was already evident, and Leon flung open the window.

Redl's room overlooked the quieter Schenkenstrasse, where Leon assumed the taxi would be waiting. The street was dimly lit, and he could just make out a dark shape that could just as well have been a night soil cart as a taxi. The ledge below the window was narrow, but Leon knew that if he had to he could make his way along it to his own room, which was no more than ten feet from Redl's.

He walked over to the writing desk, and the first thing he saw was the note from Chris Wilmot of *The Daily Mail* requesting an interview with Redl. He swore quietly in frustration at Bowler Hat's incompetence, then snatched the note and stuffed it in his pocket. There were a few other notes and receipts strewn on the desk, and he pocketed those too.

A quick glance at his Tissot pocket watch showed that he had less than three minutes to get downstairs before the taxi—if indeed it was there—left him in the lurch. He put his shoes back on and took a quick glance around the room. The desk was next to a large armoire, and for a moment Leon wondered if he should try to stuff Redl's body into the armoire rather than leave it in plain sight on the bed. Before he had time to ponder this new move, he heard voices and heavy footsteps in the corridor, and he knew that any escape at that moment would be impossible.

There was a loud knock and a voice demanded, "Colonel Redl, open the door immediately." When there was no response, whoever it was—and Leon knew instinctively that it had to be either Ronge or one of the other men that Bowler Hat had named—began to jiggle the door handle. At that moment Leon took a decision that most likely saved his life. He opened the door to the armoire and climbed in. It was empty but for one of Redl's suits and two huge fluffy bathrobes, which he managed to conceal his now trembling body behind. He left the door slightly ajar, and through the one-inch gap he had a view of the bed and part of the desk. Then the door to the room burst open and four men, two in military uniform and the others in grey suits, rushed in. He couldn't understand everything they said, but they spoke slowly enough for him to get the gist.

"Dear God," said one of the men, "we are too late. He has killed himself."

All four men moved towards the bed and then stopped. One of them, not in military uniform, prodded the body with his silver-tipped walking stick. "I don't believe so, Ronge. Unless he expertly stabbed himself in the liver from behind, I'd be more inclined to believe he was murdered."

Ronge, a tall, thin man with a bald head and neat mustache, took a closer look at the corpse on the blood-stained bed. "You are correct, General." He scanned the room and Leon held his breath. "And whoever did it must have escaped through the window just moments before."

"Or is still in the room," said the General. "Urbański, check the bathroom."

While Urbański tiptoed over to the closed bathroom door, Ronge withdrew his revolver from its holster and walked over to the armoire. He flicked open the partially closed door. Leon held his breath and closed his eyes. Whether it was the robes and the depth of the armoire or the fact that Ronge gave the interior of the armoire no more than a perfunctory glance, believing no assassin worth his salt would hide in plain sight, Leon's presence remained undetected. Urbański came out of the bathroom and shrugged.

"No one and no sign of a search. You are most probably right, Ronge. Our assassin made his escape from the window."

"Who do you believe killed him?" asked the other man not in military uniform.

Ronge shook his head. "Most likely his Russian handlers."

"It makes no difference at this stage," said the General. "There is only one course of action—only one outcome that can be made public."

"And what is that?" asked the other man.

"I'm surprised that is not obvious, Auditor Vorlíček," said the General.

"Colonel Redl must be seen to have taken his own life," Urbański said.

Ronge nodded in agreement, and Vorlíček grunted something that sounded to the still-quaking Leon like a "ja."

Without hesitation Ronge placed his pistol in Redl's right hand and twisted his arm so that the barrel went into his mouth. He placed Redl's finger on the trigger, then held a pillow over the revolver to muffle the sound and fired. There was a soft explosion, and whatever blood was left in Redl's body mixed with the grey matter already pooling on the pillow below his head. Ronge took the pillow he'd used to muffle the explosion and gingerly stuffed it under the other pillow on which rested what was left of Redl's head.

"My God," said Vorlíček, "I am surprised there is any fluid left in his body...stabbed, shot. It is most distressing."

"It would be even more distressing," said Ronge, 'if the truth were to come out. One of us will have to have a quiet word with the coroner, and General, may I suggest you contact the *Kriminalbeamte* to make sure the detectives accept our word on what has happened. I will inform the press and the relevant ministers that Redl confessed to me before deciding to take his life."

There were grunts of assent, and Urbański covered Redl's body with the duvet, leaving only his shattered head visible. Without saying another word, the four men left the room.

Thirty seconds later Leon slipped out the armoire and through the door. He looked around and began to quietly make his way towards room five. He'd only crept a few feet before he heard more footsteps coming up the stairs. He froze, knowing he'd never make it to his room or even back to Redl's room and the safety of the armoire before he was discovered. Then the door to room three opened and a familiar voice said, "Get in, quick!"

"I had a feeling we'd meet again, Mr. Reporter."

"Mata," Leon said. "What are you doing here?"

"What does it look like?" she replied. "I am in my nightgown. I was sleeping until you and those Austrian dunderheads made a racket to wake the dead. Which they clearly didn't after you killed Redl and they'd shot him. May I assume that is what happened?"

Leon looked at her in shock. "How did you know?"

"I heard Ronge and the others stomping up the stairs and banging on Redl's door. I opened my own door a crack and saw them go in. After that I simply stood outside Redl's room and listened. I heard everything. Your involvement was obvious. Now, perhaps you'd care to explain yourself, unless you are going to kill me, too."

Leon was breathing heavily. Not out of lust, though he thought Mata Hari looked particularly fetching in her sheer peignoir, but out of relief at his narrow escape, if indeed it was an escape and not an even more precarious situation. He could feel the *sica* back in its scabbard on his left ankle, and for a second he thought of using it on Mata Hari. Then he closed his eyes and slowed his breathing.

"You were right," he said. "I am not a reporter."

"That is obvious."

"I'm a freelance assassin contracted by the Okhrana to kill Redl."

"The Tsar's secret police. But you are no Russian."

"No, but my father came from that part of the world, and my family has taken on assignments from the Okhrana over the years." He knew he was getting into dangerous territory telling Mata Hari about his family. But there was something about his mysterious companion that made him feel his secret—or at least the half-true secret—was safe. "Yes," he said, "the Austrians discovered Redl was selling information to the Russians. I was sent to eliminate him before he could give the Austrians the details."

She turned and walked back to her bed. "I suspect there is more to your story, but that can wait for another occasion. I do know that at least half of what you've told me is true. Count von Hötzendorf mentioned they suspected there was a traitor operating within their espionage organization. He didn't name Redl, but I knew instinctively. There was always something a little strange about the man." She patted the bed, indicating that Leon should sit beside her. "I met him once or twice, and his attitude was one of an official who thought himself above suspicion. He lives, or perhaps I should say lived, a life far above whatever money he earned in a government post, and he flaunted his lovers at every opportunity."

"You know a lot for someone who claims to be a dancer."

She laughed. "Is any one of us who we say we are? Certainly not the two of us. But isn't that what attracts us to each other? All of Europe bristles with intrigue and trembles at the possibility of war. And Vienna, the imperial city with its lavish palaces and monuments, is at the center of it all. I am merely one of the many who take advantage of it. And why not?"

"Why not indeed," replied Leon. "Well, unless you are planning to turn me in to the authorities, I think we should take advantage—as you so aptly put it—of the situation we find ourselves in right now." Mata Hari said nothing but put her hand round his neck and pulled him backwards onto the bed.

At around three in the morning, they heard more voices and footsteps and banging of doors. There was a thump and a loud curse as if something heavy had been dropped. When things were quiet again, Mata Hari told Leon to go to his own room as she needed to get some sleep.

"Goodbye, my darling," she said, kissing him on the lips. "If you are half as good an assassin as you are a lover, then no one is safe." Leon opened his mouth to say something, but she put her finger on his lips to silence him and waved him out.[8]

---

[8] *Editorial note: It was the last Leon would see or hear of Mata Hari until he read about her execution as a German spy by a French firing squad just outside of Paris on October 15, 1917.*

At eight thirty, Leon took a shower and straightened his clothes, knowing he'd have to wear them in an hour when he would check out of the hotel and make his way to the train station.

When he went to settle his bill, the receptionist apologized for the noise and police presence and hoped Leon hadn't been too disturbed by the terrible event of the early hours. The management, Leon was told, would not be charging the other guests for their stay. When Leon asked him what had happened, he was told that it was a police matter, and no information was forthcoming.

Much to Leon's relief, no one questioned him or even gave him a second glance as he exited the hotel with his empty suitcase and got into a waiting taxi. He saw no sign of C.'s Vienna agent and had no idea how he would get back to London. He remembered Bowler Hat saying that he would be contacted once he got to Munich and so he decided that's where he'd go. He looked at a map in the station and saw that Munich was indeed the closest large city and that there was a train leaving for the capital of Bavaria within half an hour.

He bought a first-class ticket using the money he'd been refunded for the hotel room and was shown to an empty compartment by the conductor, who attempted to take Leon's suitcase. He gave Leon a suspicious look when Leon said he'd could manage himself but accepted a large tip with no reluctance at all. Before the train left the station, Leon fell asleep.[9]

---

[9] *Editorial note: I'm almost embarrassed to admit that before reading Uncle Leon's diary, I hadn't heard of Alfred Redl. Of course, once I*

began, I became totally fascinated by him. He was the son of a railway inspector who clawed his way to such prominence in a world where breeding and background truly separated the aristocracy from those who were born with a wooden spoon in their mouths. But despite the odds stacked against him, Redl rose through the military ranks to become head of the Kundschaftsabteilung, a special unit within the prestigious Evidenzburo. He was brilliant at counterespionage and, as it turns out, a master spy who betrayed his country to maintain his lavish lifestyle. Much has been said about what Redl did. Even more has been speculated about why he did it. Movies have been made, plays staged, and best sellers written (none of which I'd seen or read before writing this). You won't find any reference to the fact that the information Redl supplied was given to the British rather than the Russians in any of the exposés of his life. Nowhere other than in Uncle Leon's diary, and in some deep, dark file lost somewhere in the basement of MI6. I'm now certain that this accounts for the fact that Leon couldn't publish it during his life time. If you'd like to know more about Redl, the extraordinary traitor—now that you know the real story—I'd suggest reading Spy of the Century by John Sadler and Silvie Fisch.

Chapter 8 - 1913 Munich

The blue rider and the Black Narcissus

If the train ride from Vienna to Munich was a good way for travelers to appreciate the magnificent countryside of Austria and Bavaria—from quaint villages and rolling hills to distant mountains, cow-filled fields, and pleasant forests—Leon saw none of it. His cortisol and adrenaline levels had dropped the moment he entered the station, and exhaustion took over his body. Aided by the gentle swaying of the train, he slept eight hours until the conductor banged on the door to his compartment to tell him that Munich was the next stop.

München Hauptbanhof was crowded with commuters rushing to make it home for dinner and others meeting those who'd arrived in the capital city of Bavaria. Leon took his suitcase and made his way to the front of the station, where taxis and a few hackneys waited. He checked his wallet and found that he still had most of the money C. had given him at the club two days before— certainly enough for a hotel room, a decent meal, a few essential items of clothing, and a ticket back to London.

"Wo is der besten hotel?" he asked the taxi driver in his broken German.

"Hotel Beyerischer Hof, mean Herr," replied the taxi driver who, without even waiting to hear if that was where Leon wanted to go, pulled out into the traffic, narrowly missing a young mother pushing a carriage.

The hotel was no more than a few minutes' drive from the station, and the cabby kept up a one-sided conversation with Leon, who understood very little of what he said because of his heavy Bavarian accent. He nodded and grunted along with sufficient enthusiasm to satisfy the lunatic as he weaved his cab between carriages and cars as if he owned the road.

The Bayerischer Hof was larger and more opulent than the Klomser in Vienna. Its high barrel-vaulted ceilings, plush leather furniture, and array of guests—who looked as though they belonged at least six levels above the hoi polloi—reminded Leon that he was in the capital city of the Kingdom of Bavaria.

"What an interesting time to be a journalist in Bavaria," said the receptionist when he noticed Leon had written down his profession in the registration book. "Once the Bavarian Parliament is back in session, they will allow King Otto to be deposed by his cousin Ludwig. Then finally Bavaria will have a king who is not a little cuckoo like the last two. Perhaps you will meet him."

"I doubt that," replied Leon. "I can't imagine being invited to the palace."

"No need for an invitation," said the receptionist. "You can meet him strolling around the *Marienplatz* or one of the gardens of his many palaces. He is a very friendly gentleman."

"Really?" replied Leon, thinking back to how he'd met and saved the life of Rajah Charles Brooke on his first morning in Sarawak just over a year ago and wondering if perhaps there'd be a similar opportunity in Munich. "Well, I must send my editor a telegram to see what my assignment is. Perhaps he will ask me to interview the future king."

"Please," said the receptionist, "we would be happy to arrange a telegram for you. If you could be so kind as to write out the message and supply the address I will have that taken care of and send the answer to your room as soon as possible." He handed Leon a pad and pen.

Leon thanked the receptionist, and after considering for a minute what to say that would get him back to London without delay, he began to write: *Assignment in Vienna concluded satisfactorily. Am now in Munich. Await further instructions on getting back to London.* He addressed the telegram to Mr. Victor Mudge at 6 Upper Marsden Crescent, Victoria. "If you'd be so kind as to send this, and perhaps I shall take lunch in the hotel restaurant while I await a reply."

An hour later, just as Leon took the final sip of his Weingut Keller Riesling and wiped the crumbs from a slice of plum cake off his lips, a waiter handed him a telegram. He tore it open.

Excellent news about Vienna though our agent there seems upset. Stay in Munich. Someone will contact you with details.

Leon wondered what it was about C.'s network of

agents. So far, they'd all taken issue with him. He'd had to kill one in Mombasa and disable another in Sarawak. Fortunately, he'd done nothing to Bowler Hat other than annoy him.

Leon had no objection to hanging around Munich for a few days. It looked like a fun city, and the few women he'd seen so far were extremely attractive. The only problem was the money. He desperately needed clothes, but if he bought even the essentials, he wouldn't have enough left for more than one more night at the hotel. Still, he reasoned, that gave him two days to get money from C.'s agent if necessary, and so he left the dining room and made his way to the concierge desk to ask for the name of a decent store.

As he passed reception, the clerk who'd checked him in earlier called out. "Herr Harries, if you please." He handed Leon an envelope addressed to him with his name written in an elegant script.

Leon walked over to an alcove and tore the letter open. *Meet me at the Glaspalast at three-thirty this afternoon.*

It was unsigned, but when he lifted it up to his nose, he detected a fragrance that he knew he'd smelled before: *Narcisse Noir...*black narcissus. He tried to remember who'd worn it, and the only woman who came to mind was the enchanting Lily Tan in Singapore. Surely this couldn't be her? He crumpled the note into a ball and looked at his pocket watch. It was just after two. That didn't give him much time to shop and change.

Fortunately there were, as the concierge pointed out, shops very close to the hotel, and the *Glaspalast* was no more than a fifteen-minute walk.

At three twenty-five, freshly shaved by the hotel barber and feeling a lot less foul in his new shirt and underwear, Leon entered the *Glaspalast* and was immediately reminded of the Crystal Palace in London. The enormous two-story building with its central transept was constructed entirely of glass and cast iron and even featured an artificial waterfall in the lobby. There were large black and bronze posters that advertised an international art festival while smaller ones pointed to an exhibition of artists called *Der Blaue Reiter.* Leon had come to admire the incredible art collection in Philip Sassoon's houses, and the thought of seeing work he could discuss with his friend excited him. But not quite as much as the possibility of seeing Lily Tan.

As he stood in line to buy a ticket, he felt someone move quickly behind him, and his nose twitched. Narcisse Noir...C.'s mysterious agent had made contact. His heart began to race, but when she whispered in his ear, he knew it wasn't Lily.

"Buy a ticket for the *Der Blaue Reiter* and wait for me in between the Wassily Kandinsky and the Gabriele Münter." Most definitely female, certainly not English, and yet vaguely familiar. He bought a ticket and walked off slowly towards the salon that housed the *Blaue Reiter* exhibit.

There was something about the art that both stirred and disturbed Leon. It was unlike anything he'd yet seen and made him wonder just how many other brilliant pieces he'd missed over the years. He stood at the end of the Kandinsky section, staring at a picture of a blue rider on a white horse galloping across a field with a forest in the background.

"Does the work not move you?" said a tall woman in an ankle-length cream-colored coat. She wore a large white hat and long gloves, and a full veil covered her face.

"Not as much as your Narcisse Noir," Leon replied, feeling rather pleased with his response. She may not be Lily Tan, but Leon did not believe in wasting an opportunity.

"Hmm," said the woman. "So, someone with the ability to both kill and distinguish scents. How refreshing. Now, I need you to spend ten minutes admiring the exhibition and then leave the *Glaspalast* by the main entrance. Turn left and walk five blocks until you come to a park. The entrance is narrow and easy to miss. Buy a newspaper on the way. You will see me sitting on a bench near the exit." She didn't wait for his response.

As it turned out, finding a newspaper was more difficult than finding the park, which was accessed through a metal gate set in a recess in a high brick wall. Eventually Leon found an old man selling the local paper a block past the park. He bought one and realized how little money he had left after the clothes and ticket to the exhibition. Hopefully, he thought as he turned back towards the park, his contact would be able to take care of that.

She was sitting on a bench writing in a small journal which she held in her lap. "Open your paper and pretend to read," she said without looking up.

"Why all the secrecy?" asked Leon. "No one here knows who I am."

"This is hardly secrecy. Any intelligence officer could spot the deception a kilometer away. This is just a precaution."

"Your accent sounds so familiar," Leon said from behind his newspaper.

"That's not surprising. You and I share a homeland, or should I say you shared my homeland for a short while. I am from what we call the land of the Khoenkhoen or Namaland. The place you call German South West Africa."

"Good Lord," Leon said, putting down his paper. "Do you mean to say—"

"I'm not sure what you think I mean to say," she interjected, "and we don't have time to reminisce, so let me introduce myself. My name is Albertina Witbooi. I am the illegitimate granddaughter of Captain Henrik Witbooi, the Nama leader who fought to free my people from the German colonists."

For a moment Leon was dumbstruck. He'd heard about the famous guerilla fighter and the horrific genocide carried out by the German *Schutztruppe* led by Lieutenant General Lothar von Trotha. Ten thousand Nama and, some said, 100,000 Herero people had died in the conflict—many in the fighting, but the majority from disease, starvation, and torture in the brutal concentration camps the Germans had built to exterminate the survivors of the wars.

"I can see you've heard of the massacres."

"My brother Joe told me, and my heart is full of pain for you. It's hard to imagine that these same people we see all around us here are capable of such senseless cruelty."

"What is there to say about the mind of white people? Their insatiable greed, arrogance, and bigotry have driven the scourge of colonialism. Stealing, raping, and destroying anyone in their way. My grandfather once said, 'Victims sacrifice their lives, but perpetrators sacrifice their souls.' No, don't look up at me—pretend to read your paper."

But Leon couldn't help himself. He desperately wanted to ask her to lift her veil so he could see her eyes. Her voice was full of sadness, but he sensed a strength and determination. "How did you escape?" he asked. "Why are you here, and how are you connected to C.?"

"You have too many questions, and we have very little time before I must return to Berlin. Now, let me tell you what C. wants of you."

"Please," Leon said. "If you won't show your face then tell me a little of your background."

"I never said I wouldn't show you my face. But there's a reason I keep it covered. A person with a dark skin would attract too much attention in a city like Munich. And in any case, why should you want to see it?"

"I don't know," said Leon. "I suppose I'd like to look at the face of the person sending me off to my potential death."

"Don't be so melodramatic. You're the person who's supposed to do the killing, not get killed. I'll tell you a little if you promise not to say how sorry you are. I have no need for your sympathy."

"I promise. I realize sympathy is wasted on the past, but Joe told me the horrors of those wars and the camps, and for someone to have lived through them and escaped...well, you have to be a special type of person."

"I'm simply a survivor, and I don't believe it makes me special—just resolute. Nothing more. But if it helps you to understand me, then I'll tell you a little. My mother, one of Captain Witbooi's daughters, was raped by a German officer. I lived with my mother in Gibeon in Namaland until the conflict. When the men were all dead from the fighting, my mother and I were taken to the camps, where she soon died of starvation. Were it not for a Rhenish missionary and his wife who made me their servant, I would have suffered a similar fate to the others." She stopped for a moment and took a deep breath. "After the war they brought me back to Germany, where two years ago I was contacted—and I'm not sure how he knew about me—by a man known as Leviticus."

"Ah, Leviticus," said Leon. "He was my first contact in Cape Town. I think he has a nose for sniffing out people who can be useful, and of course he knows South West Africa."

"Yes, he does, and I know he went there after the wars looking for survivors who could help his cause. Someone must have told him about me and that I was already in Germany. The minute we spoke he sensed my hatred for the ones who wiped out my family, and he knew how to harness my desire for revenge on behalf of the British."

"But how did the missionary and his wife feel about you leaving? Did they not understand how you felt?"

"I'm sure they did. But not at the beginning. They'd been surprisingly kind over the years. I believe they thought they'd saved me. Not from the concentration camp, but from a life without the god they believed in. Then it reached a point where they were keen to get rid of me."

"Why?"

"I'd become defiant and sulky. I was no longer the

meek, grateful little servant girl, and they had no idea what to do with me. So, Leviticus's timing was perfect. He told them he worked for an agency that repatriated people like myself, and they readily agreed to hand me over. No tears were shed. Leviticus took me to London, where I received my training."

"But why on earth would they send you to Berlin and put you in even more danger?"

"Because I'd learned to harness my emotion." She paused as if deciding how much more to tell Leon. She saw genuine concern in his eyes and continued. "Berlin was the perfect location to do what I do best."

"And why is that?"

"The thing about Berlin, which you perhaps don't know, is that it is the center of decadence and debauchery."

Leon's ears perked up at the mention of debauchery. "What's debauchery got to do with your training?"

"In Berlin there are clubs where princes, counts, and generals go to partake in acts that they speak of with derision and hate when they are back in their palaces and castles and high society dinners. But in Berlin, in a dark alley between Schöneberg and Tiergarten, they all come to Der Karmin Loch, The Crimson Hole, to visit Narcisse Noir."

"And that's you? Narcisse Noir? So, that's why you wear the perfume."

"Yes, I am the irresistible *wilde*. The savage who appeals to their demented lust and hatred of the *Untermensch*. But in the end, it is she, Narcisse Noir, to whom they tell their secrets...but my story is not why we are here."

"No, I don't imagine it is." Leon immediately thought of the Heavenly Abode of the Crimson Lotus in Singapore, where he'd been given a cram course in seduction, and wondered if Albertina's training was similar. He decided to put off asking for the moment. "Tell me what C. wants me to do."

"You are to leave Munich as soon as possible and take a train to Hamburg. There you are to find and kill Yunus Tekin, also known as 'The Turk.' He is a spy who has in his possession a list of British agents that are monitoring the German naval build-up. He has informed us that unless His Majesty's Government pays him a quarter of a million pounds in gold, he will release the list to the Prussian authorities."

"Hmph."

"And what does that snort mean?"

"It means this sounds like another ill-thought-out assignment from C. It's full of holes that I will no doubt fall into."

"In what way?"

"Well, for a start, how does C. know he's not bluffing? How would this 'Turk' manage to get hold of a list of British agents? Has anyone seen the list?"

"No," she replied. "No one's seen the list, but that's not how things work. People like him can't afford to lie. He knows if he did, his business would vanish in an instant."

"That part I understand. But what if this whole thing is a ruse concocted by the Kaiser's spies?"

"That makes no sense. I would have thought that this is a simple assignment for someone of your reputation."

"As C. told me last time I saw him, nothing is simple in

the complex and clandestine web of Europe. No, I'm sorry. The whole thing is far-fetched and in any case beyond my abilities. As I keep reminding everyone, I'm an assassin, not a spy. I wouldn't have a clue how to get hold of his list."

"You have a lot of issues for one who has already accomplished a lot—or so I am told. But I had no idea you'd be so difficult."

Leon stood up, leaving the paper on the bench. As fascinating as Narcisse Noir was, he was a little weary of the whole charade and saw no reason to continue with it. Other than a few nursemaids with their young charges, the park was empty. No one was watching them. He stood in front of her with both hands on his hips. Then with the realization he looked threatening, he put them in his pockets.

"You should know that all of C.'s agents have found me difficult. There's no reason that you'd be an exception. I am difficult, and I have that reputation because I question orders that feel badly thought through. I'm sorry if I sound petulant. My frustration isn't directed at you."

"Well, I appreciate that. But in this instance, I am simply the messenger. Tell me what you need, and I'll see if I can help."

"Thank you. I'm certain you feel the same way at times. There are a few things that I need. First, I'm out of money. C. only gave me sufficient funds for a few nights. All my clothes were taken in Vienna by one of his agents."

"Whatever for?"

"He thought that if I was caught, the Austrians would know from the labels that I was British. I suppose it made sense, but it's left me in a pickle. If I'm to go to Hamburg, I will need to buy a few outfits. Second, how will I even find this Yunus Tekin or The Turk or whatever his name is? I don't know Hamburg, but I believe it's a big city."

"Those are two things I can help you with. C. knew you'd need money…." She reached into her large handbag and withdrew a fat envelop of bills. "Here, this should suffice."

Leon took the envelop and glanced inside. It was filled with 100-mark notes. More than enough for a trip to Hamburg, some new clothes, and a luxury train ride home. "Thank you," he said, slipping it into his jacket pocket.

"As to your second question, you will find The Turk at a bar called Zwei Fette Schweine in the St. Pauli district. You are to meet with him at eight o'clock the night after next. A message was sent to him that we are willing to negotiate and that a representative of His Majesty's Government will meet to verify the list before authorizing the transfer of the money to his Swiss bank account."

"And he agreed?"

"Yes, provided the meeting takes place in public. The bar was his idea. Though, how public it will be is questionable. From what we know, it is part of his operation."

"And what operation is that?"

"The Turk is the most powerful brothel owner in Hamburg, and he controls most of the prostitutes."

The thought of visiting a brothel sounded interesting. The rest sounded like pure rubbish, and Leon felt his anger welling up again. "So let me understand this," he said, flabbergasted at how infuriatingly amateurish C.'s assignments were. "I am to go to Hamburg, meet The Turk at a brothel, somehow get the list from him, and then kill him?"

"Yes, that's exactly what you need to do," she said. "I said Zwei Fette Schweine is a bar, not a brothel. He owns it, but it is on a crowded street in a busy area. You should be quite safe. After all, he wants the gold, and he can't get it if he kills you. Do you have a problem with that?"

"Bloody hell," replied Leon. "Yes, I have a problem. It's a damn suicide mission, and I have no idea how to go about it."

To Leon's surprise, she remained quite calm. "C. mentioned you'd probably think that. He told me to tell you to use the same ingenuity you used in Mombasa to kill Gubbins. I don't know the details of that incident, but C. felt confident you'd manage. Now, if you're done, I need to get to the station. My train back to Berlin leaves in less than an hour."

Leon shook his head. His exasperation was clearly wasted on Narcisse Noir. He thought back to what had taken place in Kenya. Any ingenuity he'd used at The Mermaid's Foot bar in Mombasa, where he'd saved C.'s life by killing the double agent Gubbins, was entirely in C.'s imagination. C. believed Leon had started a major brawl in the bar and used it as a diversion to get close to Gubbins and stab him. In truth, the fight that broke out between a group of soldiers and seamen had resulted from a spilled drink and had nothing to do with Leon. But C. believed Leon had initiated the fight and was so effusive in his praise that Leon hadn't corrected the misconception.

"Well," he said, suddenly feeling very alone. "Maybe you'd consider coming with me. You'll be the perfect diversion, and I'd be a lot more confident in your company."

She laughed from behind her veil. It was a sweet laugh that carried no judgement or derision, and it made Leon even more desperate to see the face of Albertina Witbooi.

"No," she replied. "I can't do that. But thank you for asking. Maybe we'll see each other again in less contentious circumstances."

"I'll come to Berlin afterwards," he said. "It's not that far from Hamburg."

"Perhaps not in distance, but your presence will put me in a great deal of danger. No, I'll meet you in London when this is over. Now, a few details for you—remember them well. The success of this operation depends on it. Once you have seen the list, you must tell The Turk that the gold has been sent to Switzerland and that you will send a telegram to your superior, who will arrange for its immediate transfer to The Turk's account. In reality you will send the telegram to C. saying that you've seen the list and it looks good. Then C., with the cooperation of his Swiss counterpart, will have the bank send a telegram to The Turk confirming the deposit."

"But even if he shows me the list of names, I won't know any of them."

"No, you won't, so your acting will have to be brilliant. Personally, I would try to kill him before you get to that part. Now, I wish you the best of luck." With that, she stood up, touched his arm, and walked out the park.

Chapter 9 - 1913 Munich and Hamburg

Out of the frying pan, into the foyer

After leaving the park, Leon walked to the Karstadt department store opposite the railway station, where he was able to replenish his wardrobe with off-the-rack clothes that fit him almost perfectly and didn't need tailoring. Like everything else in the brand-new department store, the clothes were of the highest quality and compared to London very reasonably priced. He arranged for the packages to be delivered to the hotel and strolled back to the Bayerischer Hof, where he asked the concierge to book him a train ticket to Hamburg and recommend a good hotel.

"There is but one hotel that I would recommend, Herr Harries, and that is the new Atlantic. It is the one where kings and queens and all the nobility stay when they visit Hamburg."

"Then I shall fit in perfectly," said Leon to the concierge, who from the expression on his face failed to get the irony. "Can you send them a telegram to say I shall be staying for three nights?"

"Of course, Herr Harries. If you take the early train tomorrow morning, you will be there by late afternoon. The restaurant in the Atlantic has an excellent repast, I am told."

Everything the concierge at the Bayerischer Hof said about the Atlantic was true. The hotel, which had opened just four years before to serve wealthy passengers about to embark on the new luxury transatlantic lines, was a short taxi ride from the station. It stood like some giant white palace overlooking the Alster Lake, on which small sailing boats skipped across the water in the late afternoon breeze.

The lobby was filled with elegantly dressed couples either on their way out for a night's entertainment or returning, laden with packages, from an afternoon of shopping. There was nothing casual about the scene, and yet it felt less somber than Vienna or Munich. In fact, the whole of Hamburg—and Leon hadn't been there for more than an hour—had a decidedly bright feel to it. He decided that a night on the town was called for, and after checking into the hotel—on the advice of a young bellman rather than the stiff concierge—he made his way to the Wilhelmplatz in the St. Pauli district to look for things twenty-one-year-old horny males look for.

There was no doubt that Wilhelmplatz was where the action was. The only issue was that the action wasn't the action Leon was looking for. There were restaurants and bars and young people milling around, but everyone looked sober. There were no single women displaying lewdness nor rowdies engaged in boisterous acts of fun. Leon wandered into one of the brightly lit bars and ordered a beer. When the bartender was less busy, Leon asked him if there was anywhere nearby where a man of the world might find something of interest.

"Depends on what you find interesting," replied the bartender, polishing a tall glass with what looked like an old undershirt.

"I like to think that I find people whose morals are somewhat lower than those of priests and nuns interesting," Leon said, slipping the bartender a handful of marks.

"I fully understand, *mean Herr.* My suggestion is you go to the Heinrichstrasse, where I think you will find what you are looking for."[10]

What Wilhelmplatz lacked in disorderliness, Heinrichstrasse and its surround more than made up for with drunken sailors and other assorted hooligans whooping it up as they bargained with the women in the windows. Leon began to walk down the street, marveling at the merrymaking and doing his best to avoid the stumbling inebriates. Then he stopped. *What the hell am*

---

[10] *Editorial note: Heinrichstrasse—now called Herbertstrasse—is located near the famous red-light district of Hamburg along the Reeperbahn in St. Pauli. It's infamous for its brothels and prostitutes, nicknamed Stiefelfrauen, who display their wares in the window fronts. In 1933 the Nazis, who'd outlawed prostitution, found their orders impossible to enforce in St. Pauli and erected barriers at either end of Herbertstrasse. The barriers are still up (I believe) with stern warnings that men under eighteen and women are not allowed in. In 2019 members of FEMEN, an activist feminist group, ripped down the metal barriers, but they were quickly put back up.*

I doing? he thought. If Narcisse Noir was right and The Turk controlled prostitution in Hamburg, then surely some of the women in the windows worked for him. He wasn't exactly sure how they might expose him to The Turk or how they could possibly know who he was, but it wasn't worth taking a chance. So, with a half-hearted attempt to shield his face, he walked back through the barriers and to the hotel, where he ate dinner, drank an excellent bottle of Grauer Burgunder, and went to sleep.

The next morning after breakfasting on pickled herring and smoked trout, Leon set off to get a feel for the city. On his way through the lobby, he picked up a Baedeker Travel Guide for northern Germany from the hotel store. He'd glanced through a few of Baedeker's guide books in Philip Sassoon's library and noticed how incredibly insulting they were about most countries. He remembered Baedeker's admonition that "extortion is the national hobby" of the Italians and how Greek hotels are infested with lice and bedbugs while their wines (presumably what one would drink to alleviate the horrors of the bedclothes) are "insipid and weak."

Of Germany, though, Baedeker was full of praise. Hamburg, the book pointed out, had more bridges than any city in the world and more canals than Venice and Amsterdam combined. Its people were honest and upright. Its food glorious and fresh. Baedeker had clearly not been to Heinrichstrasse, Leon decided. With the idealistic images of the Hanseatic city swirling around his head, Leon strode out onto *An der Alster*.

It was a beautiful day, sunny and warm, and perfect for sightseeing. He walked along the inner Alster Lake, admiring both the buildings and the women. He stopped off at a *schnitzel haus* for lunch and then meandered back to the hotel to mentally prepare himself for his meeting with The Turk.

He walked up to the reception desk to ask for his key and then froze in his tracks as someone called out to him.

"Schnuckelschneke!"

He turned slowly, and there under the chandelier—resplendent in a long, narrow crimson skirt and a lacy shirtwaist under a black velvet jacket, her thick blond hair piled high on her head—stood the women he'd widowed, Lady Clara FitzHatton, sister of the German empress, daughter of the late Frederick VIII, Duke of Schleswig-Holstein-Sonderburg-Augusteburg.

"Good God, Clara," Leon croaked, his throat tightening and his heart thumping against his chest.

"I never thought to see you again, you wicked boy. And especially not here in Hamburg. You and I have something to discuss, no?"

"Um," went Leon, wondering for a second whether she knew it was he who'd killed her husband at the theater.

"Don't 'um' me. You know perfectly well what I mean. You owe me an apology."

"Uh…."

"You 'um' and you 'uh' a great deal. It's almost as if you are unaware of your transgressions."

"I'm not sure what you mean."

"How boorish you act. You believe it is acceptable to ignore me after that afternoon at the Cadogan Hotel? Is that how you treat a lady? You did not call on me again. You did not write or even try to contact me. That is the behavior of a vulgarian, and I do not appreciate it. And for that you must be punished." Her voice was stern, but there was a definite twinkle in her eye.

"I'm so sorry, Clara. Of course, you're right. I just thought after your husband died so suddenly—"

"That is not an excuse. I don't give a hoot, as the British say, for my ex-husband, that *trottel.* No, you will have to make up for your rudeness. Now, for how long are you in Hamburg?"

"I leave tomorrow," he said. "But perhaps we can meet back in London?"

"No," she replied firmly, "I am not returning to London for the moment. I am visiting my cousin, Countess Hilda von Mecklenburg-Schwerin, at Schwerin Castle. Her family is away for the next few weeks, so you will join us there. I assure you between Hilda and me, your experience will be one you will not soon forget." She slapped her thigh to add emphasis to the threat.

"As tempting as that sounds, I don't think I can. I'm expected back in London the day after tomorrow."

"Nonsense," she replied. "Believe me: you can, and you will. I will not accept your excuses. Now, I have a dinner for which I must prepare. I shall be returning to the hotel at ten thirty tonight. I expect to meet you in the lobby at that time." And with that she turned and strode off towards the elevator.

Chapter 10 – 1913 Hamburg

Why fat people must be jolly

Leon had no doubt at all about what Lady Clara had in mind when she talked about making him pay for his rudeness; he still had the scars on his back from her long nails to remind him. But as terrifying as another round of sexual combat with the aristocratic hellion might be, there was also an overpowering erotic allure. Especially if it involved her cousin Hilda. He'd take care of The Turk (not that he had a clue how he'd go about it) and meet Clara in the lobby of the Atlantic at the appointed hour. And if he failed to get back to London for a week or two, then to hell with C. and *The Monocle*. He deserved a break.

At seven o'clock—the *sica* in its scabbard, firmly strapped to his left shin rather than ankle in case he was searched—Leon hopped in a taxi and asked to be taken to the corner of *Seilerstrasse* and *Davidstrasse*, two blocks from the bar where Yunus Tekin, aka The Turk, would meet him. It was too early for the revelers headed for the *Reeperbahn*, but the streets were busy enough for Leon to blend in and scope out the bar without drawing attention to himself.

Zwei Fette Schweine was, on the outside at least, smaller and more dimly lit than most of the other bars Leon had passed on the taxi ride through St. Pauli. The few patrons, both men and women, making their way in or out looked sleazy and dangerous, and Leon began to have second thoughts about the assignment. This was no "public place" as Narcisse Noir had described it. In fact, everything about the place reeked of endangerment and more likely death.

Just as he was about to turn and walk away, a large black Mercedes Corte Madera pulled up in front of the bar. A chauffer, who judging by his size and squashed nose might have been a prize fighter at some point in his life, jumped out and rushed around to the passenger side. He opened the door, and the fattest man Leon had ever seen squeezed out. He wore a homburg hat and a dark pin-striped suit that could have accommodated two regular-sized people in one of its legs. In one pudgy hand he carried a slim briefcase, and in between his fore- and middle fingers on the other was a long cigar. The fat man waddled through the door, and Leon immediately knew, while Narcisse Noir had not described his adversary, he'd found The Turk.

Leon closed his eyes and took a deep breath. As keen as he'd been a minute or so earlier to go back to the hotel, something about the fat man intrigued him. Perhaps, he thought, he'd simply negotiate without killing him, get the list of names, and then hot-foot it back to the hotel to meet Clara. He could always tell C. that the circumstances made assassination impossible, and damn his eyes if he didn't believe it.

In any other neighborhood in any other city, Zwei Fette Schweine might have been a local, packed with regulars drinking and laughing and possibly puking. But there was no conviviality in the dimly lit pub, with its faded décor and oppressive atmosphere. There was no bar as such, just wooden tables and chairs strewn around the narrow room in such a haphazard way as to make a direct run for the door impossible. If anything, the few men and women who sat around nursing beers or small glasses of schnapps looked even more dangerous and sleazy in the smoke-filled room than they had walking in from the street.

In the far corner, with his back to the wall and sitting on a chair sturdier than the rest out of respect for the girth or importance of its occupier, was the man Leon believed to be Yunus Tekin. The briefcase was on the table in front of him, and the cigar glowing under a bushy black mustache was clamped between teeth so large they gleamed like whalebones in what light found its way through the smoke. He looked up as Leon entered and nodded his bald head as if he recognized him.

Leon returned the nod. As he walked towards The Turk, his path was blocked by a blond woman in a tight red dress.

"Ah," Leon said, "as tempting as you are, *fraulein,* I have an appointment with the man in the corner."

The woman curled her bright red lips into a snarl and grabbed Leon's arm. Then with a strength that took him by complete surprise, she whipped his arm behind his back and pushed him over one of the tables. She was an expert; of that there was no doubt. Her hands travelled up and down his body searching for weapons: up the inside of both legs to his groin, the back of his waist, and under his arms. But where her expertise failed was to pat down the inside of his left shin where the *sica* lay snugly in its paper-thin scabbard. It was an unusual place to carry a knife, but then again, the *sica* was no ordinary blade, and its surprising location had escaped detection for generations of the descendants of Jacob ben Yitschak (later Isakovitsch, even later Harris, and eventually Harries).

Finally, satisfied that Leon was clean, she allowed him to straighten and up brush himself off in an attempt to regain what little dignity remained, and then she led him to The Turk's table.

"Sit down," said The Turk, pointing to the chair on the left side of his small table. "May I assume you are the representative of the British government?" His voice was low and his English heavily accented by what Leon assumed was his native Turkish. He had a smile on his face as if he were happy to see Leon.

"Yes," Leon replied, leaning forward until he was overpowered by the smell of the garlic on The Turk's breath.

"There is no need for such intimacy," laughed The Turk. "No one else here understands English and in any case they all work for me."

"I see," Leon said, looking at the mélange of characters scattered around the room. The men, he decided, all looked Turkish with their thick black hair and mustaches, while the women were either blond or red haired and Germanic in appearance. Their heads were down, though he knew they were monitoring his every move. "Very well, my name is Leon Harries, Mr. Tekin—if that's how you'd prefer to be addressed. Should we get down to business?"

"You are suggesting that there is another way to address me?"

"I've heard that you're also known as The Turk."

"Is that so? Well, let me warn you, my young friend, that anyone who's addressed me as such in the past is probably missing a tongue."

"In which case, I'm glad I asked. I imagine it would be rather difficult to negotiate without a tongue."

"You're a funny fellow," said The Turk, emitting a deep, rumbling laugh that caused some of his people to look up. "Humor is not something I expect from a British government official."

"You'd be surprised," replied Leon. "The younger generation of civil servants are a merry lot compared to the old fogies who used to populate Whitehall."

"Ha, I suppose that's good to know. So, you are the Young Turks of Britain, are you?"

"Absolutely." At breakfast on Leon's last day in Singapore before returning to London, C. had mentioned the Young Turk movement that in 1908 had replaced the absolute rule of Sultan Abdulhamid. "We're called The Britanicals." Leon had no idea why he'd just made up a nonsensical word, but it was the first thing that popped into his head.

The Turk looked at him blankly, and Leon tried desperately to come up with an explanation. "It's a combination of Britain and botanical, to signify the flower of Britain's youth."

"I've never heard of it," replied The Turk.

"Ah, well," Leon said, leaning back. "I'd be surprised if you had. We're not as forward as your Young Turks. We aren't planning a rebellion. Just a quiet takeover. You know the expression, 'slowly, slowly catchee monkey'? That's our motto."

"I am not familiar with it, but I get the meaning. So, you are one of these young Britanicals, are you? Perhaps the leader?"

"Indeed, and very much in the forefront of the movement. It's why I have been sent to negotiate with you."

"Then you're out of luck. There is no negotiation."

"I don't understand."

"The price is two-hundred-and-fifty-thousand pounds in gold paid into my Swiss bank account. Not a penny less. And because I am a fair-minded businessman, also not a penny more. Despite the elapsed time between our last discussion."

"Ah, I misunderstood. Yes, naturally the price is agreed. The only negotiation is whether the documents are in order. I apologize for the delay between discussions. Unfortunately, I was tied up in Austria for a few days having talks with Field Marshall von Hötzendorf."

The Turk snorted. "Please, you expect me to believe that you have access to Count von Hötzendorf? I hardly think so."

"I understand your reluctance to believe me, but I have a very good friend who introduced us."

"And who might that be?"

"I doubt if you'd know her."

"Try me. I know many people in our line of work."

"Her name is Mata Hari."

"You lie."

"I don't. Met her on the Orient Express from Paris to Vienna."

The Turk made a sound like a buffalo wheezing. "If you really do know her then you'll also know her real name."

"Margaretha Zelle. I also know her married name— Margaretha MacLeod—if that helps. If you require further proof, she has a birthmark on her right thigh."

"Hmm," went The Turk, twiddling his mustache in contemplation, his small dark eyes boring into Leon's mind as if he were trying to discern the truth. Then he laughed again. "Clearly you do. I saw the birthmark once, and after what her bastard of a husband did, she doesn't reveal her married name to many."

"There are things I'd lie about, but not Mata Hari. Once you meet her, she stays with you."

"What you say is true. She captures men's souls and holds them hostage. The beautiful, mysterious Mata…." The Turk gave a deep sigh and twiddled his mustache again. Then he nodded his head as if he were satisfied that Leon was telling the truth. "I have a good feeling about you, Leon. Yes, I like you. And if you feel like working for me once this is over, I could use someone like yourself in my organization. I promise you the benefits are beyond anything the British Foreign Office can provide." He looked around the room, smiling at the women.

"That's very generous, Mr. Tekin. I'd be happy to hear about them once I have verified the documents."

"Naturally. They are here in this briefcase. Open it now

and see for yourself." He twisted the tumblers on each catch and pushed the briefcase over to Leon. Inside was a manila folder, and inside the folder was a single sheet of paper on which were written a list of names and addresses. Leon picked up the sheet and The Turk grabbed his wrist. "No, no. You cannot touch the merchandise until you pay for it. Look at the names which I am sure you are familiar with."

Leon scanned the list. He'd been told nothing about the list, and he didn't recognize any of the names, but he made a pretense of scanning the sheet and pursing his lips as if he did. Then he took one of the biggest gambles of his life. "This list is fake. I recognize none of these names." He jumped up and grabbed the edge of the table as though he was about to flip it over. Someone wrapped their arm around his neck from behind, and he felt the barrel of a revolver touch the base of his spine. The Turk, who hadn't even blinked at the commotion, held up his hand and the arm was removed from around Leon's neck, although he could still feel the revolver in the small of his back. He looked at Leon carefully and then his dark eyes twinkled, and he began to laugh so hard that spittle formed at the side of his mouth.

"Ha," he said. "You are right, of course. This was just a little test to make sure you are who you say you are."

"I'm not here to play games," Leon said, trying to steady his nerves.

"Of course not," replied The Turk. "But you must understand that I could not take a chance." He reached into his coat pocket and took out a folded piece of paper which he opened and placed in the briefcase. Then he removed the old sheet, crumpled it up into a ball, and tossed it onto the floor. "Here, this is the real list."

Leon ran his hands through his hair and straightened his tie, which had shifted when whoever had grabbed him removed their arm. Then he sat down and, despite The Turk's admonition not to touch the merchandise, picked up the new list and began to examine it. The names meant as much to him as those on the false list, but he made a show of reading them carefully and staring into space once or twice as if he were trying to recall something or other. Finally, when he thought he'd given a suitable performance, he closed the folder and the briefcase.

"It appears your sources are accurate, Mr. Tekin, but how do I know that this is the only list?"

"You don't. But as I said at the beginning of our conversation, I am a businessman."

"Well, you may be a businessman, but you're also a blackmailer."

The Turk laughed. "Yes, I am. But blackmail is my business. No, there is no other list; you must take my word for it."

"Strangely enough, I do. Despite your little chicanery earlier, I can't imagine you'd have survived so long if you operated any differently. Very well, I shall send a telegram to my superior to say that the money should be transferred immediately. It is, I am told, already in Zurich, and the man I am supposed to send the message to will make an instantaneous deposit to your account. May I assume that your account details are already known to my superiors?" Leon was acting as if he were on stage at the Old Vic. It may not have gotten rave reviews in the

London press, but so far, The Turk appeared convinced. Or if he wasn't, he was giving an even better performance.

"Yes, those details were provided when I made the initial contact. There is a telegraph operator at a hotel a few blocks away. I will have him brought here and you can give him the message. The response will also be sent here. Provided it is in my favor, I will hand you the list to destroy."

"And how do I know that you won't just kill me once you have confirmation and keep the list?"

"Because you and I will take a little drive to one of my establishments—a very high class one, I might add—not far from your hotel. Don't look surprised, my boy. I would not be as effective as I am if I didn't know those sorts of details. I have people everywhere who are paid to tell me everything. Now, while we are there enjoying the entertainment, and should all go according to plan, I will receive a telephone call from my assistant. That's when I will hand over the papers, which will never have been out of your sight. Is that acceptable?"

"Sounds splendid," Leon said. Killing The Turk in the pub would have been impossible. There were too many eyes on him and too many bodyguards looking for an excuse to pounce.

While they waited for the telegraph operator, The Turk talked and joked with Leon as if he were an old friend. He told Leon about his childhood in the seaside town of Kas in southwestern Turkey and his early years in the Ottoman army.

"I was a lot thinner then, naturally, but I have an insatiable lust for food that will no doubt kill me soon enough, though I can't think of a more enjoyable way to die."

"I like food too, but personally I'd rather die in the arms of a beautiful woman."[11]

"Ha," laughed The Turk, slapping a large hand on the table. "You are a man after my own heart, Leon. Well, tonight we shall enjoy both. Wonderful food and beautiful women. Now, where is that lazy telegraph operator?"

The establishment in question was just off the Lange Reihe Street in a baroque two-story building in the St. George neighborhood and, as The Turk had mentioned, not far at all from the Atlantic. The Mercedes pulled up in front of the brothel, and the bullet-headed chauffer helped The Turk squeeze out of the back seat. Such was the fat man's girth that Leon had been forced to sit up front with the chauffer, dashing any hopes of killing his target in the confines of the car.

They were met at the door to the building by a man even larger than the chauffer, who had an angry red scar running from the top of his missing left eye to the tip of his chin. He ushered them into an entrance hall that made the lobby of the Atlantic Hotel seem like a country inn. Oriental silk rugs covered the grey marble floor, and gilt-edged chairs and tables were dotted around the room.

---

[11] *Editorial note: How prophetic those words were. Leon died in his eighty-sixth year in the arms—or shortly after he'd extracted himself from the arms—of Thelma, his long-time, and much younger, girlfriend. Whether he was enjoying himself at the time is unknown. Though after reading his diary, I like to think he was.*

There were gold sconces on the walls and sculptures of fat-buttocked cherubs on white pedestals next to urns and vases filled with fresh flowers.

"What a beautiful place," said a genuinely impressed Leon.

"It is," replied The Turk proudly. "The two floors above, if anything, are even more impressive. Unfortunately, the climb up the staircase would exhaust me for what is to come, so you will have to make do with my private lounge."

Leon followed the waddling figure down a corridor to the right of the wide staircase that led to the floor above. They came to a solid double-wooden door which the scar-faced doorman who'd led the way opened. 'Well," said The Turk, "what do you think of my suite?"

"Good Lord," Leon said, his mouth open like a carp waiting for an unsuspecting fly. "I've never seen anything like it…it's quite overwhelming."

He did not mean it in a good way, but the look of satisfaction on his host's face indicated that he'd mistaken it for a compliment. Leon shook his head in amazement at the glistening chandeliers with their dangling crystals filling the vast chamber with an eerie light that ricocheted off the huge mirrors that covered all available space on the walls and ceiling. He could see both himself and his host from every conceivable angle, and his imagination went into a frenzy at what he'd see once the entertainment began.

There were two red-velvet chaises—one larger and sturdier than the other—on a raised marble platform near a small stage on which rested a gleaming bronze bathtub and a vaulting horse. Low tables with dishes of smoked fish and lobster and hot bread in baskets had been set up next to the chaises, and a footman dressed more for the court of a French king than a German brothel stood with a silver tray holding a bottle of champagne and two glasses.

"Take off your shoes... and the rest of your clothes if you like," said The Turk, flopping onto the larger chaise. "Let us eat and drink for a while, and then I will bring on the entertainment. Then provided the right telegram comes through to my headquarters, what a marvelous night we shall have." He put the briefcase on the floor next to his chaise.

"And if it doesn't?" asked Leon.

"Then I am afraid only one of us will enjoy his time at the House of the Golden Goose, as I call this place. But why even bring that up...what can possibly go amiss at this moment?"

A whole lot, thought Leon, wondering how he was going to get the *sica* out of its scabbard and into the liver of The Turk before removing his trousers. He took a glass of champagne from the flunkey, sat on the chaise, and looked at the food. It was nearly nine thirty, and he was famished. He was fond of pickled herring, and his German sister-in-law, Anna, Joe's wife, had made it for him in Walvis Bay.

"Oh good, rollmops," he said, picking up one of the herring filets rolled around a piece of pickled cucumber. "My absolute favorite."

"Really?" replied The Turk, who'd already polished off a couple of lobsters and a loaf of the warm bread. "I wouldn't have even known what they were before I came to Germany." He picked up a handful and tossed them into his mouth like a walrus scooping up cod. "Now, of course, I can't get enough. But you have yet to tell me about yourself—"

His question was interrupted by a loud ringing. Leon looked over and saw a silver candlestick-type telephone on a small table in the corner of the room.

"Aha," said The Turk, licking the herring juice off his fingers. "Good news for both of us, or bad news for you." He signaled to the flunkey, who walked swiftly to the table and picked up the phone. He said something which Leon couldn't hear and then carried the phone, which was attached to a long cord, over to The Turk

"*Evet*," said The Turk, reverting to his native Turkish. He listened intently, his jowly face showing neither displeasure nor excitement. His eyes were fixed firmly on Leon, who did his best not to show the terror that had begun in his throat and was rapidly making its way to his bowels. And then The Turk smiled, and Leon closed his eyes in relief.

"For a moment there you looked worried," said The Turk as he placed the earpiece of the phone back in its cradle. "Come, come...you should have more faith in your secret service."

"Paranoia is the key to survival in this line of work. But I take it the transfer is complete?"

"Paranoia and a sharp stiletto," laughed The Turk. "But yes, the transfer is complete. Now I imagine you'd like the list? No, no. Don't get up." He signaled to the flunky, who walked over and took the briefcase. "Take it over to my friend and then go and get the girls." The flunky handed the briefcase to Leon and retreated to the door.

Leon took out the manila folder and opened it.

It was empty.

"What the hell?" he said, looking over at The Turk, who now had a huge grin on his face. "Where's the bloody list?"

"Right here," replied The Turk, reaching back into his jacket and pulling out the folded piece of paper. "I wasn't going to take the chance of you grabbing the briefcase and making a dash before our transaction was complete. Paranoia, as you said, my dear fellow. Here, come and get it."

Leon shook his head in feigned surprise. Then to The Turk he appeared to scratch his ankle but in fact slipped the *sica* from its scabbard into his hand. He stood up with an exasperated sigh and took the few steps over to the chaise on which his victim reclined. Before The Turk could open his mouth to yelp for the flunky, Leon grabbed the sheet of paper and plunged the *sica* into The Turk's liver.

"Paranoia and a sharp stiletto you said...well, I don't have a stiletto—only my *sica.* Will it do?" The Turk looked down in horror as Leon drew the *sica* across his body to sever the hepatic artery. It was not a good death for someone whose liver had swollen to three times its normal size from years of abuse. Nor was it easy for Leon to extract the *sica* from the rolls of subcutaneous fat. When he finally managed, blood erupted from the severed artery like a fountain. Much to his surprise, The Turk began to laugh.

"What are you laughing at?" asked Leon, wiping the

sica on the red velvet of the couch.

The Turk spoke softly. "I just remembered what a friend of mine once said: Fat people have to be jolly, for they can neither fight nor run." Then he coughed twice and grimaced in pain. His head fell back with his still-open eyes fixed on Leon who, as gently as he could, leaned over and closed them with his thumb and forefinger. He'd started to like The Turk.

Leon smashed The Turk's champagne glass and put a deep gash in the fat man's right hand and wrist. Whatever blood had not soaked into the chaise from the severed hepatic artery poured out the deep gash on his hand onto the floor. Leon's timing was perfect. The door opened and four naked women came in.

"Hurry," Leon said as the women came up to the chaise. "Get some help. Mr. Tekin has cut himself badly."

One of the women who looked a little older than the others stopped. "He isn't moving...."

"No." Leon put his hand on The Turk's forehead. "He seems to have passed out from loss of blood. Try to wrap something around his hand; I'll see if I can get a doctor."

He made it to the front door, where the large doorman stopped him with a hand that felt like a steel vice. "Let me go," shouted Leon. "Mr. Tekin has had a terrible accident. I'm going to get a doctor."

"We have a doctor on premises," said the man, tightening his grip. Then he fell to the ground as Leon delivered a crippling punch to his sciatic nerve, the move his brother Joe had shown him at the same time he'd presented him with the *sica.* This was followed by a four-fingered jab to the throat that traumatized the doorman's vertebral arteries and disrupted the vital blood supply to his brain. He passed out immediately. If any of the passers-by saw anything out of the ordinary, they pretended to ignore it, and Leon walked quickly down a side street that led to the Alster. He turned left and saw that he was no more than a block from the Atlantic Hotel.

"You're late," said Clara FitzHatton as Leon walked into the lobby. "I said ten thirty. It is now ten thirty-five. Your tardiness will be added to your long list of transgressions when we get to Cousin Hilda's *schloss*. Now, follow me up to my suite."

Chapter 11 – 1913 Schwerin castle

A formal event where clothing is optional

Just before he sat down to breakfast the following morning, both exhausted and aching from the sybaritic Clara, he sent a telegram to C. saying his assignment was complete, the list was destroyed, and he was taking a short break but would contact C. on his return to London. He didn't expect a reply, but just as he popped the last piece of apple custard cake into his mouth, a bellhop handed him an envelope. It was from C.

Excellent idea Stop Turk organization in chaos Stop Good job Stop Return to London in a week Stop C.

He'd escaped one nasty death at the hands of The Turk and his associates. Now he faced another from the combined forces of the German aristocratic sexual Olympic team. Hopefully it would be less painful.

His musings were interrupted by a small man in a chauffer's uniform who informed him that Princess Clara (he used her German title) was waiting in the car and required his presence immediately. Not wishing to add further to his list of transgressions, Leon bolted down his coffee and followed the chauffer out to a large open Mercedes where Clara sat wrapped in the fur of a dead animal.

"My apologies," he said. "I had to wait for an important telegram."

"Save your breath for when we get to the *schloss,*" she replied. "I promise you will need every ounce you have."

It took nearly four hours to get to the castle, and when Leon saw it, it took away any breath he'd managed to save for the activities ahead.

The castle lay on an island in the middle of Lake Schwerin surrounded by lush gardens with tall trees and statues and fountains. Dozens of black, slate-topped towers rose above the trees, and the myriad windows sparkled like jewels in the late afternoon sun. It was a castle out of a fairy tale.

The open car had been noisy and conversation hard to hold. This hadn't stopped Clara from prattling on about what she'd been up to since leaving London, but Leon had missed most of it. His mind was focused on what lay in store. While Clara was noisy and insatiable in her sexual demands, she hadn't as yet employed any of the Krafft-Ebing techniques that Philip Sassoon had warned him about. Leon remembered what Marcel Proust had said about aristocratic French women being "hell cats" in bed, and he hoped that, should he ever see his friend again, he'd be able to tell him that German princesses were equally dangerous.

The car pulled up through the front entrance of the castle

into the courtyard, where a perfect line of servants waited, bowing and scraping to the two grandees—or more accurately, one grandee and one jumped-up barrow boy from Spitalfields doing his best to act like a grandee. Leon nodded politely to each one, but Clara didn't even acknowledge the retainers as she glided by, her eyes fixed firmly ahead at the huge doors into the palace.

Leon followed, trying his best to look nonchalant, though the sheer scale and grandeur of the palace made him feel like a mouse in a cheese shop. The only other palace he'd been in was the Astana in Kuching, Sarawak, but the home of Rajah Charles Brooke wasn't comparable. Two Astanas could have easily fitted into the entrance hall of Schwerin castle, where gold-trimmed furniture, marble statues, and crimson curtains stood out like the symbols of wealth and power they were.

Leon's bedroom was nowhere near Clara's. Or at least he didn't think so. They'd parted at the top of the staircase with servants ushering them in different directions. He followed a smartly attired footman along a wide corridor lined with pictures of stern-looking men and sour-faced women until they came to the end of the corridor, where the footman opened the door to his bedroom.

It was a large room that smelled of cinnamon and spices. The walls were covered in teal silk on which hung paintings of noblemen on muscular charges skewering deer. There was an oval mirror over a fireplace so large it could have roasted one of the deer from the paintings. A chaise, writing desk and chair, and four poster bed completed the furnishing. He noticed a small bookshelf built into one wall, but the books looked old and stuffy and none of the titles were by Sacher-Masoch or Krafft-Ebing. Possibly the most disappointing piece of furniture was the bed itself. It was made of heavy wood, and when he sat down, the mattress felt as hard as if it had been stuffed with bricks rather than feather down. Hardly the sort of equipment for what Clara had intimated she and her cousin Hilda had in mind.

"Dinner will be served at eight o'clock, my lord," said the servant. "Is there anything you will be wanting?" He spoke in English, but accent was heavy, and he pronounced his "W's" as "V's."

"First," said Leon, trying his best to sound friendly, "I am not a lord, so call me Mr. Harries, or even Leon if you like. Second, if dinner is a formal affair, I'm afraid I don't have a dinner jacket with me. Wasn't expecting to be invited to a palace."

The servant gave a short gasp and put his right hand over his heart. "My apologies, Herr Harries. I just assumed you had a title."

"Think nothing of it, my dear fellow. Don't care for titles myself, and in any case, they don't have them where I live in Africa. Now, what's your name?"

"Gunther, Herr Harries."

"Well then, Gunther, here's a pile of marks. See if you can rustle me up a dinner jacket."

"That is not necessary, Herr Harries," Gunther said with a low bow.

"A man should be rewarded for his troubles, Gunther."

"I agree, Herr Harries," Gunther replied, snatching the money out of Leon's hand. "What I meant is that a dinner jacket is not necessary. You will not be needing it."

"I don't understand—"

"You and the Princess and Countess Hilda will be dining in the Countess's suite. From what I have been told by her maid, clothing of any sort is optional." Gunther's face went into a not-so-subtle contortion. Leon was uncertain if it was a smile or a grimace.

"You will find a fine dressing gown in the closet and, if I may make a suggestion, *mean Herr*?" Leon waved his hand for Gunther to continue. "Perhaps that is what you should wear. I shall be back at seven fifty-five to escort you to Countess Hilda's rooms. Maybe you will take a small sleep until then. I believe you will need it."

Leon stared after the retreating Gunther, who seemed, from Leon's experience, quite forward for a servant, certainly compared to the ones he'd met in Philip Sassoon's house or the Astana palace. But then again, if German aristocrats were all as insane as Princess Clara— or Lady FitzHatton, as she was known in London—then the servants were no doubt equally unhinged.

Leon went into the bathroom and took a bath in a tub that, much to his delight, had steaming-hot running water. There was a cake of soap that looked, judging by the odd hair, to have been used before. He tossed it into the bin and washed himself as best he could without soap. After drying with a towel that even his mother, who hated throwing anything away, would have gladly burned, he doused himself liberally from a bottle of 4711 Eau de Cologne, donned the heavy velvet dressing gown, and lay on the bed, where he fell into a dreamless sleep.

"Herr Harries...Herr Harries...you must wake up, *mean Herr.* It would not do to keep the ladies waiting."

Leon sat up and blinked. "You're probably right. Oh well, lead on, my good man." He stood up and followed Gunther out his bedroom and up a spiral staircase, which ended at a bronze door. Gunther held up his hand and reached into his coat pocket. "You must put this on," he said, handing Leon a silver sequined mask.

"In for a penny, in for a pounding," Leon said as he tied the mask over his eyes. He'd never been with two women at the same time, and while he was apprehensive at what lay beyond the bronze door, the electric thrill that began at the top of his head and ran down his body dispelled any foreboding of the entertainment to come. Before Gunther could raise his hand to knock, Leon shoved the door open and pushed past the startled Gunther into the oddest room he'd ever seen.

The room, at the very top of the largest tower, was perfectly round. Whatever daylight remained was held at bay by dark velvet drapes that covered the windows. It took no more than a few seconds for his eyes to adjust to the soft glow from the hundreds of candles that flickered on sconces and tall candle sticks dotted around the room. He could make out a table to his right that held food and bottles of wine in silver buckets, but it wasn't the light or the food that caught his attention.

In the center of the room was a bed, and on the bed, as naked as he was under his robe, sat the princess and her cousin Hilda. Where the princess was lithe and brittle, her blond hair held in place by a blue ribbon, Hilda, in contrast, was round and soft with red hair that cascaded over her shoulders. Leon paused for but a moment to gird his loins for what was to come. Then he dropped the robe, gave a loud 'Tally Ho!" and leapt onto the bed.[12]

---

[12] *Editorial note: As you are aware from all of my editorial asides, Leon is discreet with details, ungenerous with descriptions, and downright selfish—in my opinion—when it comes to depicting the really juicy bits of his sexual escapades. However, with Princess Clara von Schleswig-Holstein-Sonderburg-Augustenberg and Countess Hilda von Mecklenburg-Schwerin, he had not one but two changes of heart. The first because he wrote a seven-page description of the goings-on in the round room at the top of the tallest turret of Schloss Schwerin. The second because he expurgated all seven pages at a later stage. I tried my best to see through the dark blue ink he'd used to censor the piece, but all I could make out were some choice phrases and broken sentences. He must have had a rollicking time as you can see from the following, though whether the rollicking was more pleasure than pain is unclear. "Clara gave a squeal of delight when I squeezed her [what he squeezed was too difficult to make out]. Pain gave way to pleasure when Hilda finally removed the clamp [attached to what?]. Clara's breasts were the ne plus ultra, Hilda's buttocks sheer perfection [makes sense]. I let out a sharp howl [the mind whirls]. Why do you need handcuffs [why indeed?]. My God, where are you going to stick that [hopefully not in Leon]." Etc., etc. You get the picture.*

Now, while the full scale of activities that took place in the round room will forever remain a mystery, one can confidently assume that they were both stimulating and satisfying, because when Leon picks up the story, it is already December. Leon hightails it from Schwerin, and the reason he gives for his sudden departure is the disastrous fire that partially destroyed the castle on December 15. News reports claimed it was caused by a vengeful servant who'd been unfairly dismissed, but Leon said it was from a candle in the room that toppled over during a threesome so ardent and lascivious that he, the Countess, and the Princess narrowly escaped the blaze with their lives.

Chapter 12 – 1914 London

Your country needs YOU

"Good God, old bean," said Philip Sassoon, taking a sip of his tea. "Did you at least apologize to the Grand Duke for reducing his palace to ashes?"

"Never met the old boy. Clara and Hilda kept me pretty much out the way, and in any case, it was only partially burnt."

Philip smiled. "Hopefully he had good insurance."

"With a niece as crazy as Hilda and a cousin as wild as Clara, I'd be surprised if his insurance hadn't been cancelled. I'm telling you, Philip, I'm lucky I'm not headed for a convalescent home. If Krafft-Ebing was still alive, he'd be making some serious revisions to his sexual text book."

Philip gave a good-natured snort. "You'll have to tell me all over a whisky. Tea seems a slightly inappropriate beverage for the subject matter to which you allude. Nevertheless, you appear well."

"Oh, I am. Never felt better or fitter for that matter. Now, look at the time. I'm supposed to meet Smith-Cumming at his club."

"Well, it's good to have you back, Leon. You've missed the rest of The Season, but there's always next year."

It was several months since Leon had met with C. at his club, The Oriental, for his assignment to assassinate Colonel Alfred Redl in Vienna. Other than the weather, very little had changed. When he entered the Smoking Room, he found C. reading his newspaper in the same chair he'd left him. This time a fire blazed in the large hearth, doing its best to drive out the chill that crept through the ill-fitting windows of the otherwise cozy room. While London was awash in Christmas decorations, none adorned the halls and chambers of The Oriental. Leon wondered if it was because The Oriental's roots lay in the East. He asked and C. dismissed the question with a wave of his hand.

"We're not here to discuss tinsel and mistletoe. It's your tardiness that concerns me. You young fellows have absolutely no conception of time. You tell me you'll be gone for a week or two and then, low and behold, you disappear for bloody months on end. Astounding, I tell you. And up to no good, I'll wager."

Leon filled him in on the details surrounding both Redl's and The Turk's deaths, which mollified C. somewhat. "Good job with those two. The question is: what have you been up to since?"

C.'s monocle fell out when Leon mentioned his chance meeting with Mata Hari, and he went into a violent coughing fit when Leon told him about his activities at Schwerin Palace. "Good God above. Tell me you at least found out a few things that could help us."

"Not really."

"Not really? What the hell did you talk about?"

"There wasn't much talking. Some shouting—"

C. held up his hand. "Spare me the sordid details."

Leon, who hadn't planned to discuss any of the activities with C., bit his lip. "Look, C., I apologize for not getting back sooner, but I thought the invitation from Lady FitzHatton—who's reverted to her Princess of Schleswig-Holstein title, by the way—and her cousin, Countess Hilda of Mecklenburg-Schwerin, was too good to turn down. I was wrong from an intelligence-gathering perspective. But I needed a break."

C. let out a groan. "The story becomes more outrageous by the moment. You do realize how dangerous it was to see Princess Clara again? You could have easily slipped up and said something that would have made her suspect your part in her late husband's demise."

"Not much chance of that," Leon responded. "She couldn't stand the blighter, and in any case, as I said, conversation was down to the minimum."

"Damn me, but you're getting full value from The Heavenly Abode of the Crimson Lotus. I'll have to let Cassandra Collingswood know about her star pupil."

Leon grinned. He'd no doubt that what he'd learned in a single afternoon at the school for advanced sexology, aka, The Heavenly Abode of the Crimson Lotus, and its proprietor, Cassandra Collingswood, had put in him in high demand with upper-echelon society women in London and now Germany.

"Anyway, I'm back and ready for a new assignment. Do

you still want me to take out that Black Hand fellow, Colonel Dimitrijević?"

"No, I need you to sit tight for the moment. Get back to your society column. Stay in with Philip Sassoon's crowd. Things are up in the air, and they could go in any number of directions in the next few months. Taking out the most important figure in the Balkans right now could be disastrous. I'll stay in touch."

But Leon didn't hear a word from C. He wrote his column and attended Philip's lavish parties unaware of the powder keg that was about to blow. Then on June 28th of 1914, barely seven months after C. had stopped Leon from taking out Colonel Dragutin Dimitrijević, a young Bosnian named Gavrilo Princep, on the orders of Dimitrijević, assassinated Franz Ferdinand, heir presumptive to the Austrian Emperor Franz Joseph. Whether C. knew he'd blundered badly by telling Leon to sit tight is not recorded, and in any case, there was precious little he could do to prevent the terrible war he'd predicted two years earlier.

On the first weekend of World War I, in August of 1914, three thousand young British men a day signed up to join the armed forces. Leon happened to be visiting the Sir Sydney Smith pub on the Saturday, ostensibly to see his parents, but in reality to meet up with Gladys, the barmaid he'd been having an on-and-off fling with since moving back to London.

"Please don't tell me you intend to volunteer," said his mother Bryna as she replenished the pickled egg jar.

"I have to," Leon replied. "I have no choice."

"Yes, you do," Abram interjected. "If you remember, I told you this would happen. I heard from Melville that Philip Sassoon will be appointed private secretary to Field Marshall Haig at the British headquarters in France. Didn't I say the upper classes will become the officers and the rest cannon fodder? You may have been living like one of the nobility, but in the end you're still plain old Leon Harries from Spitalfields. See if Philip can put in a word for you."

"You're right, and you did say that. Philip told me about his proposed new position. But he's already an officer, and his French is perfect, so that position is made for him. In any case, I think in this war even officers will be cannon fodder. No, I'm sorry, Mum and Dad. I can't ask Philip to do anything for me. I'm going to the recruiting office tomorrow."

No amount of begging, pleading, or crying could get Leon to change his mind from doing what he felt was his duty. He left his mother wringing her hands and his father reaching for the bottle of Vat 69 Scotch and made his way back to his small flat, where he had one drink and promptly fell asleep.

Fate and the British Secret Service had a different plan for Leon. Twenty minutes before he was to set off to the nearest recruitment office, he received a telegram from C. It told Leon to report to him at precisely ten thirty. The address was number 2 Whitehall Court, flat 54 on the 8th floor.

"How do you like the place?" asked C., who sat behind a highly polished wooden desk strewn with papers.

"I didn't realize this was an office building...I always thought it was a block of flats."

"It was, and a damn posh one at that. Gladstone lived here, as did H.G. Wells, and even the man whose face graces just about every recruitment poster in England, Lord Kitchener. Although why anyone would think his ugly mug would attract young men is beyond me. Should have had the face of a young woman on the posters. 'Visit me in France' should be the caption. We'd have men joining up in the millions."

"Certainly would have worked for me," Leon replied. "Be that as it may, I was on my way to enlist when I got your telegram."

"Good for you, my boy. That's the spirit. But I can't have you do that. I'm going to need you to work exclusively for me. You've probably read the newspapers about the hundreds of German spies operating in the UK."

"I have. It seems the police round up more and more every day."

"Yes, but most of it is pure balderdash. These are times of extreme paranoia where everyone is suspicious of their neighbor. Especially if they have a German-sounding name. There are spies to be sure, but not as many as most people think, or to be honest, as dangerous as the public is led to believe. We'll catch 'em and shoot 'em at dawn, have no fear, but the real danger lies in the colonies, not Old Blighty. Do you recall Paul von Lettow-Vorbeck?"

"Wasn't he the German officer who organized the hunting party to bring the Thunder Eagles together in Tanzania in 1911?"

"At least you haven't lost your memory. You're correct, and you foiled his plans by assassinating the American Philip Krause, and Count Orlov and Baron Krissendorff. Well, it now seems Lettow-Vorbeck is playing merry hell with our boys in East Africa."

"So, you need me to deal with him?"

"No, I damn well don't. Just listen, will you, for once. What I need you to do is take out some of the biggest agitators in German West and South Africa, people who see the war as an opportunity for the Afrikaners to overthrow the British and take back what they believe is theirs. You're to head to Walvis Bay on the first ship out this week. Meet up with your brother Joe, who has been briefed thoroughly by our people. The two of you need to work together."

"Don't forget, we only have one *sica* between us."

"I didn't forget. You'll do alternative assignments or whatever Joe decides. I don't really care how you go about it. Now, good luck. Who knows how long this bloody war will last, but I will need you back here at some point. I'll stay in touch. Now, good luck, my boy." C. stood up and walked over to Leon and squeezed his shoulder in an avuncular way. Then he returned to his chair and picked up some papers.[13]

---

[13] *Editorial note: Oddly enough, what Leon and Joe did in South Africa and South West Africa between September of 1914 and November 1916, when Leon was called back to London to be given the strangest assignment of his life, is not included in the notes my son discovered in the third volume of* The Adventures of Haji Baba of Ispahan. *I do know from what my father told me, and I referred to it in* The Tailor of Riga, *that Joe carried out a number of critical assassinations in South West Africa during World War I. At some point he was captured by the*

Germans and imprisoned in Fort Namutoni, which is now a camp in the eastern section of the fantastic Etosha National Park. When I was very young, we visited Namutoni and saw the actual cell that served as my grandfather's prison for a year or two. The German authorities must not have had any idea who he was, or there's no question they'd have shot him. I have no idea what role Leon played during that time, because the notes only picked up the story when he returned to London in late December, 1916. He spent a day with his parents at the Sir Sydney Smith Pub and then met with C. at his office at Whitehall Court at ten o'clock.

Chapter 13 – 1916 London

Your assignment is to murder a monk

C. was sitting not behind his large polished desk as he had been at their last meeting, but in one of the two leather armchairs that made up the rest of the furniture in his spartan office. He was in the process of opening his correspondence, which was piled high on the coffee table between the chairs, with a thin-bladed stiletto. He looked up when his secretary ushered Leon in and indicated that Leon should take the other chair.

"Ah, Leon, my boy," said C., putting down the letter and stiletto. "A belated merry Christmas. I see the past two years or so haven't changed you one bit. You still look like the cheeky chappie I met in Mombasa in 1911."

Leon laughed. "Older and I hope wiser, but I'm in good health." He paused and his tone changed. "Which is more than I can say for our troops in the trenches. I would have been there if you hadn't stopped me. I should be there."

C. nodded. "You've performed your duty to His Majesty's Government, so stop carping. Believe me, there is no glory to be had in the fields of France and Belgium, only death. I said to you a while back that this would be a brutal war. Unfortunately, brutal doesn't do it justice. We and our allies have suffered more casualties than in all other wars combined. And it's not over yet by a long shot. If President Wilson doesn't allow the United States to join us, I'm not sure we can win this. Which is why I need your services. I take it you brought the *sica* with you? Didn't leave it back with your brother, Joe?"

"No, I still have it," Leon replied, feeling the pressure of the sheathed *sica* on his left ankle.

"Excellent. Well, what I am about to ask of you now is certainly dangerous, possibly suicidal, but absolutely crucial to ensuring our young men have not died in vain."

"Sounds like every other mission you've sent me on," Leon said and immediately regretted it.

C. looked at him for a moment and shook his head. Then he picked up the stiletto and plunged it into his leg.

Leon jumped up, pulling the *sica* from its scabbard and holding it in front of him.

"Steady on, old chap," C. said, tears of laughter rolling down his cheeks. "That not quite the reaction I was expecting. Most people simply faint when I stab my wooden leg."

"For a moment I thought you were going to stab me," Leon said, placing the *sica* back in its scabbard. "I didn't think you were going to rip into your own appendage. I had no idea you had a wooden leg."

The smile left C.'s face. "Yes, unfortunate car accident shortly after I sent you to Africa in 1914. My son was killed, and I ended up losing my leg."

"I'm dreadfully sorry about your son," Leon said. "I

didn't know about the accident."

"Alistair was twenty-four. Just about the age you are now." He looked down and his chest heaved. Then he took a deep breath and seemed to steel himself. "Well, can't be helped. Have to move on. Thousands of parents have lost their sons in the war." He pulled the stiletto from his wooden leg and placed it back on the coffee table. "Now, where were we?"

"You were about to send me to my death."

"Oh, right, and don't be so damned morbid. I didn't say you'd die, I simply said it was a distinct possibility. Hopefully you can be back home for New Year. Not that's there's much to celebrate these days." He examined the small tear in the leg of his trousers where he'd stabbed himself for a moment, then looked up at Leon. "What do you know about a fellow named Rasputin?"

"Absolutely nothing," Leon replied. "Never even heard of him."

"Very well," said C., settling back in his chair. "His full name is Grigori Yefimovich Rasputin."

"So, he's Russian?"

"Of course he's bloody Russian. What the hell did you think he was?"

"I have no idea, but the Russians are our allies, aren't they?"

"They are, though Rasputin is doing his damndest to change that situation. But I'll get there if you stop interrupting. Now, it's a lot to take in, so let's get some tea, unless you'd prefer something stronger?"

Leon would have preferred a whisky but decided he'd probably fall asleep the way C. was wont to drone on.

After C.'s efficient and very patient secretary had brought them mugs of standard British governmental brew, C. sat back in his chair and began to talk.

"Rasputin is a mystic, a holy man, a faith healer, and a thoroughly dangerous lunatic. A lot of people refer to him as the 'mad monk' but the Tsarina, Alexandra, thinks of him as a savior. She believes he's solely responsible for healing her son Alexei's hemophilia."

"Surely Tsar Nicholas doesn't buy all that mumbo-jumbo?"

"Hard to say at the beginning, but the reports are that he's starting to listen to the monk's venomous spew. Nicholas does not have the strongest intellect in the rapidly declining brain power of the Royal gene pool. That's my opinion by the way, so don't go spreading it around. The point is, many, including Nicholas's closest advisors, fear Rasputin's power is growing and that he's already beginning to influence foreign policy."

"And that will affect the war?"

"Precisely. Our agents inside Russia believe that Rasputin is urging the Tsar to make a separate peace treaty with Germany. If that happens the Germans will move all their resources on the Eastern front to the Western front. Now," C. said, holding up his finger to stop Leon interrupting again, "the Eastern Front is much larger geographically than the Western Front. It stretches from the Baltic to the Black Sea and includes most of Eastern Europe. The Western Front, on the other hand, is highly concentrated. It's only being fought in Belgium and France. Can you imagine the full force of the Central Powers, Germany, and Austria-Hungary plus their allies the Bulgarians focused entirely on the Western Front? Then even with the help of our American brethren—and hopefully they'll step in—we'd be overwhelmed."

"I understand," Leon said, once more regretting that he'd asked for tea rather than alcohol. "Well, I can certainly see why the 'Mad Monk' has to go. When do you need me to leave?"

"Stout man. The answer is right away. The navy's lent us their newest ship—and their fastest—HMS *Renown*. She's anchored off Scapa Flow, and she'll take you to a location just south of St. Petersburg, or Petrograd as the infernal place is now called. Our agents will meet you there."

"I hesitate to ask this," Leon said, "because as the Black Narcissus told me in Munich, you seem to assume my ingenuity will solve any issue at hand, but have you any idea how I'm supposed to insinuate myself into a situation where I can get close enough to Rasputin?"

"Ah," laughed C. "The 'Black Narcissus' as you call Miss Witbooi...yes, she speaks fondly of you, though I'm uncertain as to why. Probably because you didn't attack her as you have most of my agents to date."

Leon rolled his eyes. It was true that he'd killed Gubbins in Mombasa and incapacitated Stuart Grant in Sarawak. But Gubbins had been a double agent, and Stuart had tried to have Leon slaughtered by headhunters, and to his mind they'd deserved what they'd got. Narcisse Noir, on the other hand...he looked up at C. "Is she here in London? We said we'd meet up when we were both here."

"She told me, and yes, we managed to get her back just

before the Germans arrested her. Damned useful woman, but she asked one too many questions of Paul von Hindenburg when she had him trussed up like a Christmas goose. I'll let her fill you in on the details...but only when you get back.

"Now, you asked if I had an idea as to how you'll get close to Rasputin, and I do. One of our agents, a man named Oswald Rayner, is a close friend of Prince Felix Yusupov. Met the blighter at Oxford and they've been tighter than a frog's arse ever since. Your cover will be as the correspondent of *The Mayfair Monocle*...I take it it's still going?"

"Yes, I left it in the capable hands of my editor, who's managed to keep the presses running despite the war. Who am I supposed to be interviewing?"

"That part I'll leave to you, Rayner, and one of our other agents, Bertie Stopford, who'll no doubt employ his connections with the Russian nobility."

"Well, I'd better go home and pack."

"Won't work, old chap. You're flying to Scarpa Flow in one of the brand-new Bristol F-2's. Takes two people—that'll be you and the pilot—and bugger all else. Rayner will outfit you when you get to Petrograd. You're costing us a bloody fortune in new clothes, by the way."

"Forget the clothes; I'm not sure I want to fly."

"No choice. Takes too long by ship. You'll be in very capable hands. Pilot is a fellow named Frank Barnwell. He's the man who designed the plane. Perfectly safe."

"I heard our pilots have an average life span of two weeks."

"I told you before, Leon. Don't be so morbid. You're not

exactly going into action against Baron von Richthofen. No, your chances of making it to the Orkneys and Scarpa Flow are extremely high. Well, the plane's still a prototype, so perhaps I'm overly optimistic. Oh, do relax. You'll be fine. Now, off you scoot. There's a car waiting to take you to the Central Flying school at Upavon Aerodrome in Wiltshire, where you'll meet Barnwell."

Chapter 14 - 1916 Upavon, Orkney, and Petrograd

The magnificent assassin in a flying machine

The car dropped Leon off at Upavon Aerodrome in Wiltshire at just after three o'clock that afternoon. He'd missed lunch and was hungry, annoyed, and apprehensive. Leon had certainly seen planes and been as thrilled as most observers seeing the relatively new-fangled flying machines soaring across the skies. Active participation in the very act that had killed Icarus and various others over the years, however, was not on his list of must-do's. Philip Sassoon, who'd trained as a pilot, had offered to take Leon up in his plane, but the idea of leaving *terra firma* filled Leon with a buttock-clenching dread.

A friendly pilot directed Leon to a small hangar, where he found Frank Barnwell standing on a short ladder tightening a bolt on the engine of a two-seater biplane. Barnwell was a well-built man with a neatly cut RAF-style mustache. He wore grease-stained overalls and a tweed flat cap, which he worse in reverse.

"Ah," he said when Leon finally introduced himself after waiting for Frank to finish tightening whatever it was he was tightening. "So, you're Leon Harries, my co-pilot on our first long test flight to Kirkwall. Well, what do you think of the F-2?"

"Um," Leon said, wavering for a minute between a response that conveyed either terrified or distressed and opted for something neutral. "I don't know anything about aircraft, and I've never been in one."

"Then you're in for a treat," said the famous airman. "She had her maiden flight just a week or so ago. Handled beautifully, and if I can just figure out the right engine to put in, she'll be as fast as any fighter out there. This one's got a Falcon 1, but I'm going to see if a Hispano-Suiza is better on my other prototype."

He glanced at his wrist watch, which looked very much like a pocket watch with a strap. "Too late to leave this afternoon, so follow me to the mess. I'll get you some grub and a thick jacket so you don't freeze your arse off up there, and find you a place to sleep. We'll leave once it's light. Weather report is good for tomorrow, fortunately, so with any luck I'll have you in Orkney by lunch time."

Leon was too numb to speak. It wasn't just the thought of flying that terrified him or the fact that the Bristol F-2 was a prototype and had only flown once; it was Frank Barnwell himself. He was just too upbeat and brimming with piss and vinegar, much like some of the other adventurers Leon had met over the past few years. They were all lunatics as far as he was concerned. Men who didn't recognize death until it punched them in the heart.

Still, Frank was good company and entertained Leon and some of the other test pilots at Upavon with his stories about designing planes with his brother Harold and his short stint with the Royal Flying Corp's 12 Squadron. They drank beer and ate fish and chips wrapped in newspaper amidst a motley arrangement of tinsel and attempts at Christmas decorations that did little to cheer the room up. Then, despite the hardness of the army-issue bunk bed, Leon fell into a deep sleep and only woke up when Frank told them it was time to leave.

"It's about six hundred miles to Orkney, and we'll need to stop along the way for aviation spirit. This is a good test to determine the range of the plane and perhaps see what the glide time is. As I said, the weather's fine until we reach the north of Scotland, where it gets pretty dismal. But that's to be expected. The weather's always shit up there. It will be another good test for the Bristol...see how she handles in a storm. What's wrong, old bean? You look like you're about to throw up. For God's sake, turn your damn head if you're going to do that when we're in the air. I hate the smell of vomit."

The flight started off perfectly. Leon kept his eyes closed during takeoff, and when he opened them the F-2 was skimming across the treetops of Wiltshire. They flew over Silbury Hill, the prehistoric chalk mound near Avebury, and Frank dipped the wing so Leon could get a better look.

"It's the tallest prehistoric man-made mound in all of Europe," he yelled. "I'll give you a gander at some other stuff as we fly over. Wonderful to see things from up here, don't you agree?" Leon's answer was lost in the wind, but the truth was he was beginning to enjoy the sensation.

By the time they reached Swindon, Leon was positively jubilant at what he was seeing so far below the plane. He was warm enough in the thick leather jacket, and the helmet and goggles stopped the wind freezing his ears and eyeballs. Other than the odd landmark which Frank was quick to point out, he totally focused on the plane. The odd splutter and clang of the engine, sounds that made the back of Leon's neck prickle, didn't seem to bother Frank at all. He flashed Leon the thumbs up each time the plane did something that Leon was convinced it shouldn't be doing.

They stopped to top up the tanks in Huddersfield and again at Edinburgh. Frank tested the glide when they reached Thurso just before crossing the North Sea to Kirkwall in the Orkney Islands. Here the weather turned nasty, and Frank took the plane up to 17,000 feet. They were just above the cloud ceiling, but they couldn't escape the high winds that tossed the plane about like a dirigible in a gale. There was a point when Leon was so terrified he began to wonder if he should renew his lapsed interest in religion. Then suddenly the clouds parted, and he could see Scarpa Flow with the British fleet anchored in the choppy waters beneath. They landed in Kirkwall at two o'clock.

"Didn't she handle everything like the beauty she is," said Frank, patting the fuselage. "Not too nervous, were you?"

"Not a bit," Leon said. "I had every confidence in the plane and your flying ability."

"You're a dreadful bullshitter," laughed Frank. "Don't

think I didn't see you hurling your guts onto the runway as you got out. Anyway, this is it for me. End of the proverbial line for today. I have a few things to tinker with to get her ready for the flight back tomorrow morning."

"Thank you," said Leon. "I was a little nervous, I must admit...." Frank laughed. "All right, I was a lot nervous. Not that I have anything to compare it to, but it was an experience I won't soon forget."

At that moment a lorry carrying five sailors appeared at the end of the runway and made its way towards the plane. Frank waved at them. "Now, if I'm not mistaken those chappies are here to pick you up for wherever it is you're going next. I have no idea what you do, but good luck with whatever it is." He withdrew a sealed envelope from his jacket and handed it to one of the sailors who'd jumped down to assist Leon. "It's for your boss. Make sure he gets it as soon as possible." Then he shook Leon's hand and opened his toolbox.

The captain of the *Renown*, Commander Hugh Sinclair, read the letter that Frank Barnwell had delivered. When he was done, he tore it to shreds and turned to Leon, who was still trying to warm up from the launch ride to the new battlecruiser.

"Smith-Cumming," he said to Leon, handing him a large glass of Scotch, "has informed me of your mission. It is a dangerous undertaking but vital to us if we are to win this bloody war. I will, of course, provide any assistance I can, though short of getting you there without being hit by a torpedo from a German submarine is probably the best I can promise."

"I was under the impression that the Germans were back home licking their wounds after the Battle of Jutland."

"Yes, well, it depends which newspaper you read, I suppose. The truth is Jutland was a tactical victory for the Germans...we lost more ships and twice as many sailors as they did. For us it was a strategic victory in that we've managed to retain our blockade of the Atlantic. But it was not the outcome Admiral Jellicoe wanted. It was no Trafalgar, that's for certain." He poured Leon another Scotch and then sat down at his desk. "Right now, Admiral von Tirpitz, who commands the German High Fleet, is turning his focus to submarine warfare, and while the *Renown* has been fitted with 550 tons of armor plate, submarines are still a damn nuisance."

Leon shuddered. Having just avoided a fiery death in the air, was he now to be faced with a cold and watery one under the North Sea? Why, he asked himself, did he always end up in these situations?

"C. has asked me to give you my own perspective on where we stand so that you fully appreciate what he has tasked you with doing," said Sinclair, oblivious to Leon's anguish.

Leon gave an inward groan. He hoped this wouldn't be anything like one of C.'s lengthy ramblings that normally left him numb. In this he was pleasantly surprised. Sinclair was articulate and informative but also concise and to the point. His summary of where things stood with the allied armies and what could happen if the Americans did not enter the war—or if Russia struck up an alliance with Germany—was both frightening and factual and left Leon in no doubt as to how vital his mission would be to the eventual outcome.[14]

The *Renown's* launch took Leon to a deserted beach near what is today known as Sosnovy Bor, fifty-one miles west of Petrograd. He had to wade through three feet of icy water to the shore, and by the time he got into the car, which was waiting just beyond the tree line, he felt as if his legs were about to fall off.

"Sorry about the uncomfortable greeting, old man," said his fellow passenger in the back seat, who introduced himself as Oswald Rayner, "but these days it doesn't pay to take chances. Here, remove those shoes and wrap this fur around you and have a decent slug of this vodka. Hate the stuff myself, but it's kept millions of peasants from freezing in this godawful climate for centuries."

Leon took the proffered flask and swallowed a large gulp and then another. The vodka did the trick—not necessarily in warming him up, but rather in taking his mind off his freezing limbs. "Thank you," he said, handing the flask back to Rayner. "But why all the secrecy about my arrival? We're still allies—Russia and Britain—or am I too late?"

---

[14] *Editorial note: Leon's observations appear to be entirely accurate as to the character and abilities of Admiral Sir Hugh Sinclair. At the end of WWI, he became Director of British Naval Intelligence and in 1923 succeeded Sir Mansfield Smith-Cumming as head of the secret service. In 1938 he bought Bletchley Park with six-thousand pounds of his own money. Bletchley Park became the principal center of allied codebreaking during WWII. Sinclair died in November 1940.*

Rayner laughed. "Not at all. Timing is perfect. It's the situation that's a complete cock-up. You'll have more than enough time to learn the intrigues of the Russian Court and take your shot at Rasputin. What we don't want is for my immediate boss, Samuel Hoare, to know more about your assignment than we decided to tell him. He's a pompous ass and has the job because our ambassador, George Buchanan, believes he is of the right class compared to the rest of us. Hoare shows his face, and we hide ours, and that's how the work gets done. If he gets wind of what you're here to do, he'll cause a ruckus and derail everything because it 'won't be done by the book.' Hoare has been jawing with a right-wing politician named Purishkevich, who's mentioned a plot by a few of the nobles to kill Rasputin. Hoare thinks it's a harebrained scheme, which of course it is, and that the Tsar is better off just banishing the mystic. So you can imagine how it would go down if he knew of C.'s plan."

"Well, if the nobles plan to kill him, surely that's better than one of us."

"Naturally, but those aristos couldn't organize a piss-up in a brewery. Their attempt would be so disastrous it would most likely end up getting Rasputin declared the next Tsar of Russia. Trust me, this is a far better idea. C. tells me you're the best there is."

"I suppose I should be flattered, but my gut feel is that he simply has no one else to turn to. Quite frankly I feel as if I need the perseverance of Sisyphus. Each day is another uphill battle with a large boulder. Every assignment is about stopping one thing or ending another, and the outcome is always inconclusive."

156

"I don't doubt it, but you're not alone. It's the clandestine world we operate in. Nothing is ever really certain. You just have to keep doing what you do and hope for the best."

Leon thought Rayner to be a most pleasant and entertaining companion, and as the car clattered along the dirt road already covered with a light dusting of snow, he told Leon about his childhood in Staffordshire as the son of a draper and his time at Oxford, where he studied languages and met Prince Felix Yusupov. "Whom," he said to Leon, "you will get to meet very soon. Capital chap...richer than Rockefeller by a bloody mile. But he's a good egg and vital to the success of your mission, as you'll no doubt find out."

"In what way?"

"Hoare believes him to be one of the fellows involved in the plot to kill Rasputin. The prince has not confided in me to date, and I haven't pushed him on it yet. But between you and me, it's the sort of mad caper he's likely to be at the center of. Him and some of the younger grand dukes. They're all barmy as a box of frogs...now, here we are on the outskirts of Petrograd. Don't get too despondent at what you see. It's a pile of shit in winter but a grand city in summer and spring. Wide boulevards, palaces, magnificent stores—rather depleted, I might add, with the war and all that—and brimming with insurrection as more and more Russians become disillusioned with the Tsar and the war. I don't think there's any stopping the coming revolution, but if your mission is successful, it will give us the time we need for our American cousins to jump in. Please God they do."

"Both C. and you seem worried that they won't come to the party, and I'm not sure I understand why. Surely they're on our side?"

"I'm not overly worried, but as I said, in our game nothing is certain until it is. President Wilson pledged the United States' neutrality in 1914 and he's been holding fast ever since. Don't forget America has a huge diversity of European citizens. The Irish Americans hate the British, the German Americans are on Germany's side, and the clergy are tearing their hair, banging their Bibles, and preaching against the war. However," he said, holding up his finger to emphasize his point, "when German subs sank the *Lusitania* last May and several US ships bringing supplies to England, sentiment began to shift. So, my guess is they'll be in it up to their eyeballs before long. But we must operate as if they'll stay home. So you see, you cannot fail."

Leon stared out at the streets of Petrograd. It was just after six o'clock, but already darkness enveloped the city. The street lamps did their best to dispel the gloom, but few storefronts were lit, and Leon could sense the despair that Rayner had mentioned. The boulevards were wide and the buildings impressive, but uncertainty and oppression hung over the city, and there was no disguising it. It could just have been his imagination, but most of the people he could see from the car windows looked sullen and angry.

"You look pensive, old sport," said Rayner.

"Oh, just trying to understand the situation."

"Oh, perish the effort. Don't even try. It's not worth it. All we can do is try to preempt, and if not, deal with things as they come up. And now, talking of coming up, we're just about at your hotel, the Grand Hotel Europe. You're having dinner with Bertie Stopford at eight. I assume you know who he is?"

"C. mentioned him but no more than that."

"All I'll say is that he's a colorful character. But I'll let him fill you in on the more flamboyant aspects of his life. Scintillating company, I assure you. By the way, there's a full wardrobe for you in your room. You'd better come up with an excuse for why you're dressed as you are when you check in, or they'll sling you out on your bottom."

Chapter 15 –1916 Petrograd

The devil appears before dessert

Unlike most hotels that use the adjectives *grand* or *royal* or *splendid* in their name but aren't, The Grand Hotel Europe was truly *grand* in every sense of the word. The lobby, with its pink and black checkerboard floor, was *grand.* The crystal chandeliers that lit up the stately gold-ringed columns that lined the way to the reception desk were *grand.* The Christmas tree and statues of saints were *grand.* In fact, the only thing that wasn't *grand* was Leon, who took the edge off the *grandness* in his salt-encrusted leather flying coat and wet shoes.

"Ah, Mr. Harries," said the overly dignified receptionist, giving Leon what felt like a haughty sneer, "we have been expecting you. I believe the wardrobe you sent ahead has been unpacked in your room, and if you ring for the butler once you have settled in, he will be happy to donate your current outfit to one of the many homeless peasants who roam our streets."

"No, no, I'm keeping this," replied Leon. "Got a trifle wet when I crashed my plane into the sea just off the coast. Had to swim the rest of the way in. About a mile, I think. But no matter. The salt adds character to the clothes. Just direct me to the room, my good man."

"My apologies, Mr. Harries. I had no idea you were an airman. Do you wish me to call a doctor?"

"Oh no, just a little frostbite. I've had worse. Flown a few important missions...you know, doing my part to keep the Hun in check."

The receptionist raised one eyebrow in a look that said *I'm not sure I believe you.* Petrograd was awash in adventurers and ne'er-do-wells with all sorts of dubious stories of derring-do. But then the eyebrow settled back in place. Leon was, after all, a paying guest and acquainted with Mr. Stopford, friend of the Royal Family and even the Tsar's aunt, the Grand Duchess Vladimir. He'd give him the benefit of the doubt. He handed Leon the key to his room, which was one flight up. "I believe you are the dinner guest of Mr. Stopford this evening. Evening dress is recommended."

Leon's room was every bit as luxurious as he'd imagined it would be. The walls were cream-colored silk embossed with gold fleur-de-lis, and paintings of bored-looking men on horses and pulchritudinous women in sleds draped in furs stared down at him. He wondered if anyone who owned a hotel or a palace, had ever seen the works from *Der Blaue Reiter* movement or any pieces of modern art for that matter. Swapping out their stodgy paintings for the colorful and spontaneous paintings he'd seen in Munich would add some life to their establishments.

His new clothes, including a splendid Astrakhan coat,

had been carefully hung in the closet, and his dinner jacket and shirt with a dizzying array of studs and cufflinks lay on the bed like a corpse. A young—and Leon thought, very attractive—maid exited the bathroom and informed him that his bath was ready and would he like assistance? Her accent was Slavic, but her words were annunciated and her voice husky.

"I'd appreciate that," Leon said, suddenly feeling his old lusty self again. It had been three months since he'd been with a woman, and he thought the maid would serve as a suitable end to the drought. "Should I undress here or in the bathroom?"

"Wherever you wish, sir," she said, knowing exactly what he was implying. "I shall call your butler Gregor to assist you." She gave him a smile and scurried out the room before Leon could tell her he didn't need Gregor to wash him. He was in and out the bath just as Gregor, an elderly man with an obsequious expression, knocked politely on his door. Leon informed him that he could return in half an hour to help him with his bowtie that, despite the many times he'd worn one, he still couldn't manage to tie.

At eight o'clock—for he'd timed it precisely—Leon was escorted to a table in the l'Europe restaurant. The table was positioned so that it gave its occupants a perfect view of the entire Art Deco-style restaurant. Most tables were occupied, and no guest looked out of place as they sat eating and drinking beneath palm trees in large copper pots under the watchful gaze of Apollo in his chariot, the centerpiece of a huge stained-glass mural. The room was oddly silent as if no one wanted anyone else to overhear what they were saying, and few diners even gave Leon a second look.

Bertie Stopford was already seated. He was a small, middle-aged man with a still-handsome face lined not with worry, Leon thought, but experience. He wore a dark-blue velvet dinner jacket with a diamond-encrusted star on his lapel and greeted Leon warmly with a neatly manicured hand and the softest skin Leon had encountered since squeezing the rump of the Countess of Mecklenburg-Schwerin.

"Aren't you the dashing assassin," said Bertie as Leon sat down. "Although I should probably say 'correspondent,' should I not, Leon? You don't mind me calling you Leon, by the way?"

"No," whispered Leon. "I don't, but I'm shocked you'd refer to me as an assassin in the middle of a busy restaurant."

"Oh, pish tosh," said Bertie with a dismissive wave. "One shouldn't give a fig's nostril about anyone here. They're so busy worrying just how they're going to get their jewels out once the Bolsheviks take over, they aren't focused on much else. Other than getting drunk and fornicating like stoats, of course."

Leon looked around at the diners. The men were in evening dress or military uniforms decked with medals and awards. The women were all in long silk dresses, the colors more subtle compared to those worn by the socialites at some of the parties he'd been to in London. He couldn't speak as to haute couture in the rest of

Europe as his only other experience with high-society women had been in Schwerin Castle, and both ladies in question had been naked at dinner time.

"Do you know some of the people in the room?" he asked Bertie.

"Good God, yes. Slept with many of them. You see that fellow over there? The one in the blue uniform with the magnificent beard? He's Prince Alexei Dashkova."

"I do," said Leon, doing his best not to stare at a man who looked like his idea of a Russian prince. "What about him?"

"He and I have been lovers for years. He's hung like a horse. Here, have some water or you'll choke."

"I'm fine," replied Leon. "My apologies for reacting like that."

"Think nothing of it," laughed Bertie. "Things are different here. Certainly, compared to England. In Petrograd anything goes. It's very like the collapse of the Roman Empire if you know your history." He didn't give Leon an opportunity to reply. "When the barbarians are rattling the gates, the wealthy turn their minds and bodies to unspeakable acts of decadence and debauchery, for all hope is lost."

Leon nodded his head. He liked the idea of debauchery and wondered if he'd have the opportunity to participate. "Well, then it seems as if I have arrived just in time for the fun part."

"A boy after my own heart," laughed Bertie. "Now, let's order, and I'll give you the lay of the land so we can plot your moral turpitude." He signaled the waiter, who rushed over and bowed. Bertie ordered in Russian. "You do like caviar, don't you?"

"I do, though I can't say I've eaten a ton of it."

"Excellent. Tonight you'll try both Beluga and Sevruga, and you can tell me if you can taste the difference Next, I've ordered *kulebyaka.* It's a very intricate pie made with *vyaziga*, which is the spinal cord of the sturgeon."

Leon blanched. "I'm not sure I'd enjoy spine."

Bertie laughed, "I assure you it's delicious and so damned expensive that most Russians can only dream of eating it. But tonight, we're not going to spare any expense, for tomorrow, as they say, we may well die."

"Hopefully not," Leon replied as the waiter poured them each an ice-cold glass of vodka to accompany the caviar. Both the Beluga and Sevruga were delicious, but he couldn't really discern any difference in taste. "I intend to do what I came to do and then get the hell out of here. Though I wouldn't mind a little action before I leave."

"That's the spirit," Bertie quipped cheerfully. He gave Leon a flirtatious smile. "But tell me, Leon, you and Philip Sassoon are well acquainted?"

"Yes, he's a good chum, though I've hardly seen him over the past few years. I was sent to Africa by C. and only got back a week or so ago. Do you know Philip?"

"Intimately, though like you not for the past three years. If you don't mind me asking, were you two…uh…?"

Leon laughed. "No need to say it…no, we are simply good friends. I am strictly heterosexual."

"Pity," Bertie said, patting Leon's hand. "You're rather dishy. But good to know up front. I shall have to be satisfied with my prince." He gave a disappointed sigh. "Oh well, we shall just have to find our fun someplace other than in bed." He sat back and took a sip of his replenished vodka, which he drank like water. "Let me give you a quick rundown of what Russia is facing at this very moment, and you'll understand why you were called in."

"Oswald Rayner gave me some idea, but I'd appreciate your perspective."

"Good, though perhaps I should fill you in on my situation first. Technically I'm an antiques dealer."

Leon looked puzzled. "Really? I thought you were one of C.'s agents."

"Ah, but I am. My 'legitimate' business gives me access to some of the most powerful people in Russia and thus intimate knowledge of the machinations of the court and nobility. I offered my services to C. on one of my trips back to London, and he snapped me up just like that." Bertie clicked his fingers to emphasize the point, confusing the waiter, who rushed up to refill his vodka glass. "I like to think of myself as an antiques expert whose hobby is espionage rather than the other way around. As I said, most of the people in the room this evening, or the ones home in their palaces or on their estates, have seen the writing on the wall. I simply offer to help them get their money or jewelry out the country, and in return they impart anything I want to know. It's very useful."

"I imagine it must be." Leon had drunk two glasses of vodka and was feeling a little light-headed. He refused a third from the attentive waiter.

"You may as well get used to the vodka," said Bertie. "People here virtually bathe in the stuff. By the way, in case you're wondering, I'm the one who found out about what the Mad Monk's been up to. Other than the Tsarina, he numbers countesses and duchesses amongst his most ardent devotees. He tells them everything and they in turn spill the beans to harmless old Bertie." He stopped suddenly and looked to his right. "Talking of which...."

A deathly silence had descended on the restaurant as if the devil himself had entered the room, and all eyes turned towards the entrance. An extremely tall, thin man with long, greasy hair and a shaggy beard had walked into the dining room. He was accompanied by two women who, in contrast to his dull and rather grubby looking habit, were decked out in glamorous gowns. The man's eyes, dark and sunken, scanned the room as if daring anyone to hold his gaze. The eyes stopped for a moment on Bertie and Leon. Bertie nodded his head in acknowledgement and Leon shivered. "That," said Bertie, "is Rasputin himself."

"He certainly looks like everything he's cracked up to be, and damned scary at that. But who are those two women with him?"

"They," said Bertie, lowering his voice, "are the Black Princesses, Milica and Anastasia, daughters of the King of Montenegro. They're married to two brothers: Grand Duke Peter Nikolaevich and Grand Duke Nicholas. They're the Tsar's first cousins once-removed. The princesses are the ghastly pair who introduced Rasputin to the Tsar and his family."

"And they're called the Black Princesses, you say? I imagine for no good reason?"

"Spot on, old sport. The two of them are into the occult and mysticism and other evil-eye rubbish. As thoroughly dangerous a pair of harpies as you're likely to meet."

"Perhaps I should," said Leon, a note of excitement in his voice. "They'd make damn interesting subject matter for readers of *The Mayfair Monocle*." A movement to his left totally took the wind out of his enthusiasm. "Good God," he said to Bertie, "I think Rasputin is coming over to our table."

"Oh, Jesus," whispered Bertie as the tall monk approached. "You're right. Look, he doesn't speak English, so don't even try to talk to him."

Rasputin stood at their table for a minute before he said anything. His eyes were not black, as Leon had originally thought, but a blue so dark they looked like deep wells and were hypnotic in their intensity as they focused firmly on Leon. He did his best to hold the monk's gaze, but he couldn't and looked down at his plate. Rasputin gave a soft chuckle and began to speak to Bertie in a voice that emanated directly from his stomach. Leon had no idea what he was saying, only that Rasputin continued to look at him as he spoke to Bertie. Bertie responded to Rasputin, and while he sounded confident, Leon noticed his hands twitching. After a short conversation the monk turned and walked back to his table.

"That was rather terrifying," Leon said, taking a gulp of his vodka, which had magically been refilled while he'd been concentrating on his plate. "What the hell did he want?"

"Nothing good, I assure you," Bertie replied. "I've met him before on numerous occasions, and while I don't believe in his hocus-pocus, some of the things he appears to discern are uncanny. He didn't know who you were, but he said that he doesn't trust you and thinks you mean to harm someone important."

"Christ, how the hell would he even think that?"

"God alone knows, but that's why people believe he has mystical powers. I told him that you were a journalist here to interview some of the nobility about their social lives and nothing more, and that's why we were having dinner—so I could get to know you and introduce you to the right people. It seemed to satisfy him, but who knows. I think we'd better get your social calendar up and running as soon as possible."

Leon looked over at Rasputin and the Black Princesses. They were drinking and laughing, but every now and then the monk looked over at him, and it sent a shiver down his spine. Conversation during the rest of the meal did nothing to assuage his anguish. Bertie told him how the dreadful death rate of Russian soldiers—almost two million to date—was causing army leaders to question the war and that some divisions had already mutinied. Strikes were frequent, and even the *Duma* had been temporarily dissolved on the orders of the Tsar. "Advised, of course, by Rasputin," said Bertie. "But while all this is going on, I assure you the nobles still believe Mother Russia will come out of the turmoil just as she has in the past."

"I thought you said they were so worried that they're smuggling out their possessions," Leon said.

"That's true. But it's because any Russian worth his salt likes to hedge his bets. They believe in Mother Russia with their hearts but not their heads. Of course they're still throwing lavish affairs. There's one tomorrow evening at Vladimir Palace and you're invited. My good friend, Grand Duchess Maria Pavlona, is thrilled to have you as her guest. Bring your notebook. Anyone who is anyone will be there."

"Hopefully not Rasputin," Leon said, taking a quick peek at the monk's table.

"God, no." replied Bertie. "They hate the bastard. And believe me, if they knew what you're here to do, you'd be the guest of honor."

Chapter 16 – 1913 Petrograd.

A night to remember and a morning to forget

It was snowing lightly the next morning when Leon awoke with an awful hangover. He stared out the window at the traffic grinding along on Nevsky Prospect and wished he'd stopped drinking after his f fth glass of vodka. He ordered coffee and a hardboiled egg, ate, threw up, and then went back to sleep until just after noon.

It was still snowing but his headache had vanished, and he thought a walk would clear his head. As he got up to go to the bathroom, he noticed than an envelope had been pushed under his door. Inside was a hand-written invitation—or what looked like an invitation—on heavy stock paper. The problem was it was in Cyrillic, and he had no idea who'd sent it or when it was for or if indeed it was an actual invitation. He vaguely remembered Bertie saying something about the Grand Duchess Vladimir inviting him to a dinner and assumed this was it.

Dressed in one of the charcoal suits that he retrieved from the wardrobe and pulling on the ankle-height fur-lined boots that immediately made his feet sweat, he grabbed the heavy Astrakhan coat and an odd-looking fur hat and made his way downstairs to the lobby, where he asked the concierge if he could translate the invitation.

If the concierge was impressed with the invitation, his face did not betray it. "It is an invitation from the Velikaya Knyaginya Vladimir—or Grand Duchess Vladimir, as you say —inviting you to dinner at her palace on the banks of the Nevka. The dinner is at eight o'clock this evening."

"Excellent," said Leon. "Would you arrange for my dinner suit to be pressed?

"Of course, sir," replied the concierge, "and I believe there is a gentleman over there who is looking for you."

Leon turned around and saw Oswald Rayner near one of the pillars. He gave Leon a friendly wave.

"I must say you look a damned sight better than you did after your icy dip in the ocean yesterday. The clothes fit rather well."

"This is probably the fourth time that the British Secret Service has had to outfit me, so I would imagine they have my measurements pretty much down by now."

Oswald laughed. "I also heard you had quite the dinner. What do you think of our Mad Monk?"

"Quite possibly the worst person I've ever encountered, and from what Stopford told me, the bastard is onto me."

"I wouldn't go that far. My guess is that he was after Stopford rather than you. Rasputin knows Bertie has the ear of many of the Romanovs and other notables, so he does his best to intimidate him on every occasion he gets. Mostly to show who's in power. Still, we need to keep vigilant."

"Why?" Leon sounded alarmed.

"The Tsar and Tsarina are jumpy as hell, and if Rasputin puts a flea in their collective ear about some foreigner in the company of Stopford or me, then you never know what can happen. You could be arrested as a spy and sent to some place in Siberia."

"That's not a comforting thought."

"No, it isn't, but you can relax; that's unlikely. In any case the Tsar has his hands full trying to make sure that not every soldier under his command is needlessly slaughtered or hell-bent on murdering him and his family. Now, if you're up to it, let's get a spot of lunch and I can fill you in on your dinner tonight."

The snow had let up and even the sun had come out, and the walk to the small restaurant (which Rayner said lacked atmosphere but served great food), while skin-numbingly cold, was almost pleasant—almost, because just about everyone they passed looked hungry and sullen, not just the many wounded soldiers but the women and children who stood shivering on every street corner begging for food.

"They look at us in our fancy coats and all they see is the bourgeoisie stealing and cheating the poor. Wages have been increased but it hasn't helped. Lines to get essential products are longer than ever, and when they get to the front of the line, what few products there were are gone."

Rayner continued the conversation over large bowls of borscht with hard-boiled eggs, steaming potatoes, and *pampuska*, which Rayner explained were sweet, yeasty buns from the Ukraine. "Corruption, which under normal circumstances is awful, is now even worse, if that's possible. The only thing that's cheap and available is vodka, so the place is teeming with angry drunks. And yet the wealthy still have everything, as you'll find out tonight."

"I certainly get the bleakness of the picture," said Leon, wiping his beetroot-stained lips with his napkin. "You told me a little yesterday and Bertie reinforced it last night. All I can say is that this place, with the possible exception of the jungles of Sarawak, seems more dangerous than any I've been in so far. Personally, I don't care who takes over, provided they do so once I'm gone. And I'd like that to be sooner than later. In fact, I'd like to do what I came here for as quickly as possible and then leave."

"Can't say I blame you. I'd feel the same way in your position. You're certainly someone who speaks his mind. It's refreshing, and the Ruskies love that sort of speak. So, don't hold back is my advice. Right ho. Well, I take it Bertie filled you in on just who the Grand Duchess Vladimir is?"

"Not really, other than she's rich."

"Indeed, she is. The 'grandest of the grand duchesses,' they call her. Her jewelry collection rivals that of the Nizam of Hyderabad, and Bertie has been secretly taking pieces out of the country for her. He can tell you about that at some point. I only mention it so you understand the tight bond between the two of them, which is immensely useful to us. The duchess is the eldest daughter of the late Grand Duke Frederick Francis II of Mecklenburg-Schwerin—"

"Did you say Mecklenburg-Schwerin?"

"Yes, why do you ask?"

"Because I spent a month at Schwerin Castle just before the war."

"Excellent. Then you'll have something to talk about."

"I doubt it. Most of the time I was busy with her niece, Countess Hilda."

"When you say 'busy'...."

"I mean in the grossest sense of the word. Hilda and her cousin Princess Clara of Schleswig Holstein drained every ounce of energy—and fluid—from me.'

Rayner held up his hand. "You need say no more, old chap. I am not one to judge the excesses of my fellow man, but it seems you're perfectly suited to the degeneracy of Petrograd. Now, let me explain who else will be at the dinner."

Leon took a sip of tea—he'd declined vodka—and leant forward. "Should I take notes?"

"Not necessary, although I'm sure you'll be doing that tonight. First, the man I mentioned yesterday, Prince Felix Yusupov. My good friend from Oxford who is married to the Tsar's niece, Irina. I've told him about you—not your mission, of course—and he'll look out for you. Or so he says. You never know with Felix. He's a little flighty. Then there's Grand Duke Dmitri Pavlovich. He's the Tsar's first cousin and like you, apparently, a roué of the first water. Yusupov and he are close, and they both believe the Tsar must get rid of Rasputin. There's a good chance they can get you to Rasputin, but double check with Bertie. He'll be there, of course, together with a number of young countesses and other notables. You are the well-known British correspondent of *The Mayfair Monocle* and nephew of the Earl of Lisburne. Bertie has already told the Grand Duchess of your status."

"I've no idea who the Earl of Lisburne is," Leon said.

"And no one at dinner will either. That's why we chose it. Lisburne is a Welsh lord and Harries is a good Welsh name, even though you're as much a Welshman as I am Chinese. All you need say is that you left the Lisburne family estate in Trawsgoed—that's in Ceredigion, Wales—to go to the diamond fields of West Africa. The very mention of diamonds will have them jumping all over you, which no doubt some of the women will do in any case. Now," he said, reaching into his pocket and taking out a red leather box, "here is something to hang from your dinner jacket." He opened the box and took out a diamond and ruby encrusted medallion in the form of five-pointed star and handed it to Leon. "That is the Most Illustrious Order of King Shaka of the Zulus."

"Good Lord," exclaimed Leon, examining the piece carefully. "You don't say."

"The King died in 1828, by the way, so don't go saying he pinned it on you. It is awarded for bravery in the face of overwhelming odds by Shaka's descendants in case anyone asks."

"Not sure anyone would believe a Zulu would give a white man a medal. It isn't as if we'd done them any favors. Who is the current king anyway?"

"No idea, but no one at the dinner will know either. The diamonds and rubies are real, so don't lose the damn thing. I borrowed it from the ambassador's wife and need to return it tomorrow before she finds out. And now let's get you back to the hotel so you can prep for tonight."

After once again enlisting the help of old Gregor to tie his bowtie, Leon stashed the *sica* in his trunk and walked down the stairs to the lobby. It was a minute past eight, and Bertie, who to Leon's surprise had a permanent suite at the Grand Hotel Europa, was already waiting for him.

"Oh, my dear," he said to Leon as he gave him the once over. "Don't you look dashing, and with the Illustrious Order of King Shaka positively dripping with blood and balderdash from your lapel."

"It's the Most Illustrious Order," laughed Leon. "The more common Illustrious Order is given to any old Tom, Dick, or Harry. Now, perhaps on the way you can enlighten me as to what to expect tonight and whom I should get close to who can get me near Rasputin."

The Vladimir Palace was on what Bertie referred to as "the palace embankment," overlooking the Nevka River. It was not that far from the hotel, but the streets were slow with horse-drawn vehicles trying to make their way through the snow, which was now driving hard enough to make vision difficult.

"We'll have to get a sled to take us back at this rate," said Bertie. "It'll be impossible to drive in an hour. So, as to tonight...I suggest that you get as chummy as you can with both Prince Yusupov and the Grand Duke Dimitri.

The more I think about and listen to the rumors tossed about by my friends, the more I believe that they are the chief instigators in the movement to get rid of Rasputin. I know Oswald mentioned your name to Yusupov, but understand both he and the Grand Duke may be a little cold at first. They'll warm up once they see you at a few social affairs during the next few weeks."

Suddenly the car slowed as the driver attempted to stop and succeeded only when the car slid into the curb. "What ho, driver!" yelled Bertie. "We have invitations...no need to crash the party." He laughed at his own joke. "Here we are, the Vladimir Palace. Not overly impressive from the outside but quite magnificent once you enter."

It was hard to see the outside of the palace through the snow, but it looked to Leon like a giant sandstone-colored brick with windows. The chauffer, whose expression indicated he'd rather be near a cozy fire than risking his life on the treacherous street for two upstarts, opened the door and slipped into a dirty pile of snow. Bertie yelled something to him in Russian which sounded more like "you idiot" than "are you OK, my good man?" Then he took Leon's arm and rushed him to the portico, where a liveried footman stood to take their coats and hand them off to another flunky, who led them up a white marble staircase.

The staircase was lined with huge mirrors decorated with finely painted flowers that burst into life as they caught the light that bounced off the chandeliers and massive lamps. Every surface of virtually every object in the hall and up the stairs was gilded, and the whole appearance made Leon feel as if he were inside the hall of an elven king. If Schwerin Castle made the Astana (residence of the White Rajahs of Sarawak) look like a hovel, then the Vladimir Palace did the same for Schwerin Castle. He did his best to appear nonchalant and unimpressed, but his open mouth and wide eyes betrayed him. Bertie dug him in the ribs. "Don't look too awe struck, old boy. They'll fling out on your ear if they suspect the blood in your veins is a shade less than blue."

The flunky showed them into what Bertie said was the Raspberry Room. The walls (appropriately, given the name of the room) were a dark burgundy and covered in paintings of landscapes rather than portraits of glum-looking relatives. But it was the guests who stood beneath the Murano glass chandelier that really made Leon take a deep breath and wonder just how in God's name he'd managed to insinuate himself into such august company.

There were only three other men, two dressed in military uniforms and the other in a dinner suit. The dinner-suited young man was talking to a very elegant older woman wearing a tiara of diamonds and pearls more brilliant than the myriad necklaces and bracelets worn by the other women.

"Grand Duchess," said Bertie, giving a low bow, "may I present the Honorable Leon Harries, who as I mentioned is here to observe Russian nobility for his society column in *The Mayfair Monocle*.

"She speaks English," Bertie whispered to Leon. The Grand Duchess extended a slender hand encased in a long white glove. Leon, who'd learned the art of kissing a lady's hand correctly while on board the SS *Gwalior* on his way to Mombasa, took it gently and brought it up to his lips.

"Enchanted, Your Highness," he said. "What an honor it is to meet such a distinguished and beautiful woman."

There was a collective gasp from the rest of the room at Leon's flagrant shattering of protocol. Silence ensued and even Bertie rolled his eyes in horror. Then the Grand Duchess laughed and patted Leon's cheek. "A young man who speaks from the heart—how wonderful. You are a flatterer, Leon, if I may call you that. But I appreciate it."

"It is I who am flattered to be here this evening," Leon replied, feeling extremely pleased with himself. "And of course you may, Your Highness."

"Good," said the Grand Duchess, taking his arm. "And now let me introduce you to my other guests." She led him around the room making introductions to Prince Yusupov, who gave Leon a friendly wink and asked if Leon was going to secretly take notes during the dinner for his column and should he be careful of what he said?

Leon laughed. "No, I won't need notes. My column is more about observations of behavior rather than interviews or even quotes. So, speak freely. I won't attribute anything to you without your permission."

Grand Duke Dimitri Pavlovich shook Leon's hand politely. "I am not in the habit of dining with newspaper men, but your friend Bertie and Oswald Rayner have assured me that you are aboveboard."

"I too can assure you that I am. I have managed to gain the trust of the people I mix with, and no one so far has taken issue with what I write. I hope you will feel the same way."

The Grand Duke nodded and turned away to talk to one of the women. The other soldier was a Russian General, Abram Dragomirov, who positively snarled at Leon and turned his back without saying a word.

"Poor man has just returned after suffering a heavy loss on the Northern Front. He distrusts the British for some reason, and newspaper people even more so," said the Grand Duchess quietly. "Don't think badly of the general. The press has not been kind to him when reporting his failures. Now, let me introduce you to these lovely young women."

The women in question were far more effusive in their greetings than the men. Leon was pleasantly stimulated as the ladies tittered and one or two raised their eyebrows. But it was Princes Irina Yusupova that held his attention. She was tall and slim with hair as black as a raven's wing, and in contrast to the lavish pieces of jewelry that hung off most of the other women, she wore a simple chain of tiny diamonds. At first she seemed shy, but when Leon kissed her hand, he heard a gasp, and her hand lingered in his for what felt like a minute but was no more than a few seconds.

"I believe you are acquainted with a relative of Irina's—and mine as it turns out."

"Perhaps I am mistaken, Your Highness, but I don't believe I have met other members of the Russian aristocracy before," replied Leon, hoping to God she wasn't going to say, "You remember dear Count Orlov aboard the *Gwalior;* you're the man who stabbed him in the liver." But her face betrayed nothing. Then Princess Irina laughed.

"Oh, she's not Russian. The Grand Duchess is referring to our German cousin—a very distant one of mine but a close relative of hers—Countess Hilda von Mecklenburg-Schwerin. The Grand Duchess received a rather explicit account of your time with Hilda and Princess Clara at Schwerin Castle. They said if you ever made your way to Russia, we should acquaint ourselves with you. Oh no…my dear Mr. Harries, are you quite well? You have gone extremely pale."

It took Leon no more than a few seconds to recover. "Oh yes, Countess Hilda and the princess, of course. I was lucky to enjoy a visit to Schwerin when they were at the castle, though I can't possibly imagine what activities could possibly need explicit accounting. They all seemed very innocent."

At this rather pathetic display of inexactitude, even the Grand Duchess laughed. "Oh, poor Leon. There is no reason for discomfort. I don't believe anyone at least since the great Giacomo Casanova has enjoyed a reputation amongst European nobility like yours. The letter came a few years ago and I'd all but forgotten it until dear Bertie mentioned your name. I dug it up and re-read it. I do hope you don't mind me sharing it with friends." A number of the other young women had gathered round the visibly flustered Leon, but it was Grand Duke Dimitri Pavlovich and Bertie who rescued him from further discussion.

"May we borrow this gentleman for but a moment?" said the Grand Duke to the women. He didn't wait for a reply, and grabbing Leon's arm he yanked him to the other side of the room, where they were joined by Prince Yusupov.

"We are all men of the world," said the Grand Duke. "But clearly you have skills and abilities, judging by the little I know of your dalliance with the Mecklenburg-Schwerin woman...."

"Don't forget the Schleswig-Holstein voluptuary," said the Prince.

"Yes, yes," the Grand Duke said in a tone that suggested he wasn't happy at being interrupted. "The point is: why do you have this outrageous and dare I say preposterous prominence amongst women?"

Leon nodded and lowered his head as he considered what to tell them. He settled on tactical honesty as the best course of action. Then he looked the Grand Duke squarely in the eye.

"First, it is true that I have managed to provide some succor, and to a degree, pleasure to a handful of aristocratic women—women who, for the most part, feel neglected and abused by husbands whose interests lie not in their own bedrooms but rather in borcellos or the boudoirs of their mistresses."

"You sound like Rasputin," said the Prince with a dismissive flick of his hand. "Only he claims he is helping them achieve spiritual enlightenment rather than pleasure. The two of you would get on like a palace on fire."

"I'm not trying to emulate him in any way. He sounds like a despicable lech who takes advantage of women." Leon gave a snort.

"And you don't?" said the Grand Duke, rolling his eyes.

"Certainly not. I do not approach the women. They approach me."

"I find that hard to believe," Prince Yusupov said. "You're hardly what I would call a 'catch,' as you British say. Or is it different in Wales, where I have heard the sheep are more appealing than the men?"

It took Leon a moment to recover from the insult. His first instinct was to tell Yusupov that for someone who resembled an undertaker's assistant, he was a fine one to talk. But both Rayner and Bertie had made it clear that the prince would be a useful ally in getting close to Rasputin, so he laughed as if he weren't in the least offended.

"You do not give women enough credit, Prince Yusupov. In my experience women are less taken in by looks as they are by technique. And I assure you: what I perhaps lack in the former, I more than make up for in the latter."

The Prince smiled. "Not a bad answer, eh, Dimitri?"

"A slick answer, indeed, but an empty one without proof. Are you a sportsman, Harries?"

"In what way?"

"Do you care to take a small wager?" asked the Grand Duke.

"I'm not entirely certain what we're betting on, but if it is what I think it is, then no, I don't bet on that. It would be taking advantage."

"My God, you are a cocky one. You think the prince and I would be at a disadvantage."

"Not at all," said Leon, very unsure where this was going. "I was referring to the women. I don't wish to take advantage of any woman."

"Come, come," the prince said. "Believe me, when it

comes to the women present in this room, the only disadvantaged person would be you."

That was all Leon needed. "Very well," he said, sounding quite icy. "I'll do it."

"Excellent," said the Prince. "I'll wager one of my Fabergé bonbonnieres that you don't end up with any of the ladies present tonight."

"And I'll throw in one of my golden jeweled sabers," said the Grand Duke.

"I accept," replied Leon, who hadn't a clue who Fabergé was nor what a bonbonniere was (although he assumed it had something to do with bonbons). "And I in turn will wager this order I proudly wear on my chest, which was given to me by the current King of the Zulus for bravery."

Bertie, who knew that the "award" belonged to the Ambassador's wife, cleared his throat. "Gentlemen, gentlemen. This has gone too far. Let us forget the wager and just have a good meal and enjoy the splendid company without demeaning these wonderful women or ourselves."

"Nonsense, Bertie," said the Grand Duke, patting Bertie on the back. "This fine fellow has made his bed, and now has to sleep in it. Mostly likely by himself." He laughed at his attempt at humor.

"I assume your wife is not included in the wager?" Leon asked Prince Yusupov.

"You're an insolent swine," replied the prince. "In a hundred years my wife wouldn't be caught dead with someone like yourself. However, as we have a rather modern marriage, you may include her all you like. Now

I see the Grand Duchess is indicating that dinner is to be served."

Leon was seated to the left of Grand Duchess Vladimir and to the right of a young woman who was introduced as Countess Anastasia Hendrikova, a lady in waiting at the royal court. She was friendly and her conversation smart if slightly dry, but her interests, much to Leon's dismay, lay more in the teachings of the church than the seductive intent of the foreigner to her right. At one point he looked around the table and caught the eye of Princess Irina, who gave him the subtlest of smiles. He smiled back and then saw the prince, who was seated at the other end of the table, give him a supercilious look. Leon didn't need much motivation when it came to *affaires de coeur,* but the smug look on the prince's face on top of the sheep insult made him determined to take his chances with Princess Irina.

Fate, as it turned out, had a far more curious direction in which to point its fickle finger, and that night Leon found himself not in the arms of the young princess but in those of her aged relative, the Grand Duchess Vladimir, aka Maria Pavlona of the House of Mecklenburg-Schwerin.

It was towards the end of the dinner, just before the fruits and nuts were served and the roast grouse was an indigestive memory, that the Grand Duchess leaned over and whispered to Leon. "It is too dangerous to go back to your hotel tonight. The snow has piled up, and even a sleigh will struggle through the streets. You will stay here, and I will have you taken home in the morning."

"That's awfully kind of you, Your Highness, but I came with Bertie—"

"Don't worry about Bertie, you silly boy. He has his own plans. In fact, if you'd been more attentive during the course of the evening instead of focusing on Princess Irina, you would have noticed that he left shortly after the venison pie. He and I spoke about you staying here before dinner, so there is no issue. Now, I am about to kick everyone else out. It is late and I need my rest. When everyone leaves you will wait for me back in the Raspberry Room. You will find cognac and cigars for your enjoyment, and when I am ready, I will share a night cap with you."

She squeezed his thigh suggestively in case he'd failed to understand her true meaning and then clapped her hands. The other guests, who were accustomed to the Grand Duchess ending a meal abruptly, immediately stood up and began to file out the dining room. Leon made a pretense of walking out with them but stopped when Prince Yusupov put a restraining arm on his. "Bad luck tonight, my friend. I shall expect that medallion in the morning."

"The night isn't over, Prince. Perhaps I shall send for that bauble you put up instead."

The prince laughed. "I very much doubt it, but as you say, the night is not over, and miracles do occasionally happen." Then he turned and followed General Dragomirov and the Grand Duke down the staircase.

Just as Leon was about to make his way to where he thought the Raspberry Room was, he sensed someone slip something into the side pocket of his dinner jacket. He looked round and saw Princess Irina with two other young women, but they did not look his way. He put his hand into his pocket and felt a folded slip of paper. He was about to pull it out to read when a young lady's maid beckoned to him from the opposite side of the landing. He walked over, trying his best to appear insouciant, and followed her as she disappeared behind a heavy silk curtain.

The maid held open a hidden door to a subtly lit corridor which led to a narrow staircase. He followed her up the stairs until they came to another door. At this point she knocked quietly, gave him a bow, and retreated back down the stairs.

It wasn't that Leon was naive when it came to just what the Grand Duchess Vladimir had had in mind when she squeezed the top of his thigh. What he hadn't clearly understood was how physically challenging a night with the richest woman in Russia would be. It took all his energy and a strict adherence to the lessons he'd learned at The Heavenly Abode of the Crimson Lotus before the Grand Duchess finally let out a satisfied yell and kicked him out her bed. "You are quite the stallion, Leon, but I'm exhausted. Dress quickly and then leave me. My butler will organize transport for you back to the hotel."

Leon blew her a kiss, but she was already asleep with an expression on her face that conveyed either satisfaction or perhaps morning gas. He couldn't tell. He dressed as best he could in the darkened room and then quietly opened the door, where he found the same lady's maid who'd led him up the secret staircase.

"Good morning," he said pleasantly. "I believe the butler has organized some form of transportation to get me back to the hotel."

"Shh," hissed the maid, holding a finger to her lips. She turned and walked quietly along the marble corridor to the main staircase, where another servant met them with Leon's coat and hat and ushered him quickly down the stairs to the main entrance.

There was a dark blue sled with two snoring horses and a driver wrapped in fur. The driver nodded to Leon but didn't bother to open the door. Leon grimaced at the thought of an open-air ride to the hotel, but at least there were heavy furs to cover everything but his face. He was so busy thinking about what had happened the previous night and whether the prince would cough up the Fabergé bonbonniere and the Grand Duke the saber that he failed to see that the driver had gone past the hotel until the sled stopped at what appeared to be a smaller version of the Vladimir palace.

"This isn't the hotel," yelled Leon. "You've got the wrong address." The driver, who did not understand a word Leon was saying, sat stoically facing forward. As Leon stood up to give him a shove, the door to the building opened and two Cossack soldiers in long blue coats and fur hats walked swiftly to the coach, ripped open the door, and grabbed Leon.

He was too shocked to put up much of a struggle as they dragged him into the building. Then fear and anger overcame the shock, and he began to kick and swear and threaten them that should they loosen his arms or he'd severely incapacitate them. But he may just as well have been a rag doll. They held him in a vice-like grip as they proceeded down an elaborately decorated corridor until they came to another door, which they opened and shoved him through so that he fell onto the hard marble floor.

"Yeow," Leon yelped. "I shall report this to the British Ambassador. You can't kidnap a British citizen." He picked himself up and was just about to attack them using the secret moves his brother had taught him when the *sica* wasn't at hand, when another door opened and a stern-looking woman in a long black dress and white apron came in. She held a small pistol in her hand, which she pointed at Leon.

"Remove your clothes," she said in heavily accented English.

"Who the hell are you...and I damn well won't remove my clothes."

The women nodded to the Cossacks, who grabbed Leon's arms once again. "Then," she said, "I will remove them for you."

Dispensing of clothing from reluctant guests was obviously one of her skills, and within a minute Leon was standing on the curiously warm marble floor naked as he'd been a little earlier when the Grand Duchess unceremoniously pushed him out of bed.

"Now," said the woman, "go through that door into the *banya.* He is waiting."

Leon looked back at the Cossacks, who stood to attention, and then at the woman who had retrieved the revolver she'd stashed in her apron pocket while undressing him. She pointed the gun at the door to the *banya*—whatever that might be—and indicated that Leon should enter. He shook his head in frustration and then, steeling himself for whatever fiendish torture lay in the *banya,* he opened the door. The stern woman quickly closed it behind him, and he found himself in an oven.

The room was filled with heavy swirling steam, and Leon thought he'd gone blind. Then he heard a loud thump followed by a grunt. He waved his hand in front of his face to dissipate the steam, and what he saw forced his testicles to retract high into his sternum. Then his stomach lurched, and he almost threw up in horror.

Sitting naked on a wooden bench being thrashed with what could have been a small tree by an equally naked woman was Rasputin.

Chapter 17 – 1916 Petrograd

A mystical revelation and a wasted opportunity

For a moment Leon and Rasputin stared at each other, and Leon realized that Rasputin's eyes were pale blue and not quite as dark as he'd thought in the restaurant. Not that the color made his gaze any less intimidating.

The monk patted the bench next to him and said something to Leon in Russian. When Leon didn't move, he repeated what he'd said, and the woman whom Leon recognized as Anastasia—one of the Montenegrins, the sisters whom Bertie had referred to as the Black Princesses—put down the small tree.

"He is telling you to sit down," she said in English. "He says you have nothing to fear." Rasputin nodded and said something else, which the princess translated. "You have nothing to fear...today. He speaks no English, so I will translate."

Leon sat down and glanced at Rasputin. In truth he'd rather have been examining the princess, who was beautiful and voluptuous, but the monk's stare was magnetic, and Leon couldn't turn away.

Rasputin began to talk quietly and slowly, pausing every now and then to allow the princess to translate. "You should think of the *banya* not just as a way to cleanse the body but also the soul. As the steam draws the filth out of your flesh aided by an application of the birch twigs...." The princess picked up the birch and gave Leon a sharp cut on his shoulders.

"Christ," he yelled. "Leave off, you crazy—' He caught himself from resorting to a word he seldom used.

Both Rasputin and the princess smiled. "Good, it's a bad idea to call a princess anything else," said Anastasia. "So, too, will the heat and the steam remove those thoughts that defile your mind."

Rasputin held up his hand and moved it slowly in front of Leon's face. Then he began to intone something that sounded liturgical, which the princess did not translate, and Leon felt his mind drifting. He'd watched a hypnotist perform at one of Philip Sassoon's parties, and at the time he had bragged to Philip that no one would ever be able to mesmerize him. And yet here he was, totally naked in a hot oven with a beautiful princess equally *in disabile,* falling under the spell of a madman with an awful-looking penis.

Rasputin put down his hand and Leon's mind returned to its previous terrified state. The monk smiled again and began to talk. "He says he needs no tricks to see what is in your mind. It was obvious from the moment he saw you in the hotel with that degenerate Albert Stopford."

"Who?" asked Leon before realizing that Bertie's real name had to be Albert. "Oh, you mean Bertie "

The princess translated what Leon had said, and

Rasputin grunted something and shook his head. "Rasputin said you act like a fool, but he knows you're not. He understands exactly what you are here to do, and it won't work."

"And what precisely is that? If he's referring to my observations of Russian nobility for my newspaper column, then everyone knows that?"

As the princess translated what Leon had said, Rasputin snarled and grabbed Leon's wrist. He began to talk quickly and harshly.

"He says perhaps you are a fool after all. But do not assume that he is one. You are here to convince the Tsar not to seek peace with Germany."

"That's rubbish. I have no intention of seeing the Tsar, who I heard is at the front in any case. I am a correspondent from London visiting Petrograd."

Rasputin let go of Leon's wrist and shook his head. Leon noticed spittle leaking out his mouth which joined the sweat already saturating his beard. Then Rasputin began to speak again in what felt more manic than before.

"Rasputin says it doesn't matter whether you admit it or not. He knows the truth and so he will explain to you why he believes you are wrong to try to persuade the Tsar to stay in the war."

"Well, I'd like to hear what he says, but it's a little hot in here. Do you think we can go somewhere cooler?" Leon did not like the way Rasputin's eyes were rolling around.

"No," said the princess, not even bothering to ask Rasputin. "You need at least forty minutes in the *banya* before we jump in the frozen pool in the back, or you will not get the benefits." She picked up the birch branch and struck him again, but this time less harshly, and he felt a pleasant tingling sensation.

"Fine," said Leon. "I'll listen, but you can forget the frozen pool. Whatever body parts haven't been roasted in this furnace by then are not going to get frostbitten as well."

The princess gave a low chortle and indicated that Rasputin should continue. "I am but a *muzhik*, a peasant born in Pokrovskoye in Siberia. People here call me *starets* even though I am only a monk by self-proclamation and not ordained. Many people, including the Tsarina Alexandra, believe I can perform miracles. But I am not a prophet. Except of course to those who choose to see what I can do by the pure power of my suggestion, which I assure you is greater than you imagine."

"Why are you telling me this?" Leon asked, beginning to think that the only time villains normally confess the truth is when they're about to kill you.

"Because if you understand me, you will realize my motivation has nothing to do with the power or money or sexual acts that my enemies accuse me of. Although in truth I enjoy those immensely. And why shouldn't I?" To underscore his point, he gave the princess's rump a squeeze. She smiled and gave him a vicious cut with the birch branch that caused him to twist his shoulder and purr like a cat.

"Ah, yes," he continued. "Some people have accused me of being a *Khlystry*."

"I don't know what that is."

"It is a sect that believes in flagellating themselves. It is outlawed here in Russia." The princess said this without bothering to let Rasputin explain. "No, Rasputin prefers someone else to flog him." She gave Rasputin another hard swat with the birch branch, which elicited a similar response to the one he'd displayed before. For a minute Leon considered asking her to give him another cut just to see what all the fuss was about, but remembering the first one she'd given him decided against it.

Rasputin continued and Leon could sense the earnestness in his voice. "It is a source of great puzzlement to the nobles. How can an ignorant peasant achieve what I have achieved when no court-appointed priest or doctor has been able to cure the Tsarevitch of hemophilia?"

"Well, if you're not a saint and it's not a miracle, then I'd like to know how you did it."

"Easy," replied Rasputin, tossing back his shaggy and extremely greasy mane. "I told his mother to keep him away from the doctors who gave him the new wonder drug *aspirine*. The minute the Tsarina listened to me and forbid the doctors to be anywhere near him, the boy started to get better. It was simple observation. Whenever he was given *aspirine* he seemed to bleed more. I don't know why. I am no scientist. Although I probably know more than any of those driveling idiots." Rasputin rambled on for a bit about inequality and the evils of wealth and power when it was used to suppress the underdogs. All of it seemed reasonable enough to Leon, who didn't think he had a choice but to listen.

Leon was starting to get confused about his feelings for the Mad Monk. Rasputin was a far different character than had been described to him by C. or Oswald Rayner.

He was clearly insane. Certainly devious. But evil? That he felt less convinced of the more Rasputin spoke.

He thought about what both Joe and his father had told him about finding out just enough about a subject—time and place being the critical factors—to make it easier to carry out the assassination. Getting emotionally involved in their lives added extraneous issues that blurred focus. He knew he had to get out of the *banya* quickly before he actually began to like the crazed cleric.

But Rasputin wasn't done. His voice had gone up an octave, and what spittle had dribbled out his mouth was now flying around the room mixing with the steam. "The degenerate nobility believe that no peasant is capable of appreciating anything that exists in a world outside of servitude. How can someone who lives in a cold wooden hut in the middle of Siberia even understand what fine wine is? Or warm clothes? No, all we are capable of is slaving in their fields or mines so they can continue to live lives of elegance and indifference. While our hands bleed and our spines twist from the work, they dance and buy baubles from the jeweler Fabergé."

Leon's ears pricked up at the mention of Fabergé. Perhaps whatever it was that Prince Yusupov had lost to him in the bet would compensate for the scalding he was currently undergoing.

"For centuries," continued Rasputin, "they have seen us as lesser beings, as swine or cattle if you like. To labor on their behalf. Even to die on their behalf."

"And yet here you are enjoying that very lifestyle that you decry," Leon said, wondering where all this was leading.

"Pah," exclaimed Rasputin. "What do you know? With every sturgeon egg I eat, every glass of sweet wine I wash it down with, every baroness and countess I defile with my filthy peasant body, every nobleman I cure with my magic and mystical gifts, I prove to these villains that everything they have been taught since the cradle is like the bilge in the bottom of a rotting hulk. Their time is almost up."

"And what do you think, Princess Anastasia?" asked Leon. "After all, you are one of these very people he seems to hate."

Rasputin looked at the princess as if he understood that Leon's question was directed at her. "Me?" she said. "I am married to a Grand Duke of an empire that will soon be swept away in revolution and from a small country that will soon be swallowed up by a more powerful one. What do I care for anything but the church and this?" Much to Leon's horror she reached for Rasputin's penis, which fortunately remained flaccid.

Rasputin cackled and moved her hand away. "So why do I wish the war to stop? I said the nobles believe it is our duty to die for them, but the numbers are so overwhelming that even some of them are becoming concerned. But their concern is without substance. Your friend Yusupov has given over a few rooms in his palace to the wounded, and other *dvoryane* supply bandages."

"Very commendable, I'm sure," said Leon, and Rasputin snorted when the princess translated. "But why would breaking the treaty with England and France and joining Germany prevent more deaths? Surely the Russian army would then simply be dying at the hands of their ex-allies?"

"Your ignorance is overwhelming," replied Rasputin. "No, a German-Russian alliance would end the war and save millions of lives. England and France would surrender immediately, and we need the soldiers for the coming revolution."

"But the proletariat who will take part in the revolution...surely they will see you as part of the old order?"

"Once again," said Rasputin, "you display stupidity beyond my comprehension."

"Steady on with the insults there, old chap,' Leon said. "I could throw a few your way that you wouldn't like."

Rasputin ignored him. "Even amongst the working classes there must be leaders. Every group needs to have one person in charge feared by the rabble. And there is only one person who fits that profile: me. The man who will lead the new Russia is the very man who brought the old one down."

Jesus, thought Leon, *if this someone doesn't kill this lunatic soon, we're all bloody doomed.* The dregs of respect had vanished in Rasputin's tirade.

"Anyway," said Rasputin, licking his thin lips, "enough of this for the moment. You and I will meet again, and I will instruct you how to speak to your superiors about me. Now, why don't you have sex with the princess?" Leon looked at her in amazement as she translated Rasputin's words and then jumped up as she made a grab for his genitals.

"Love the idea," he said, "but a little shagged out after a night with Grand Duchess Vladimir. You know how it is."

"Very well," said Rasputin, giving Leon a dismissive wave. "You typify the youth of today. No stamina. You may go, but I shall send for you again."

Yes, Leon thought, *but next time I will have my sica.*

When he was safely back in his room at the hotel, he remembered the note that someone had put into his pocket just as he was about to enter the lair of the Grand Duchess. He opened it up and his heart began to race.

I will send for you tomorrow night. Irina.

Leon climbed into bed and fell into a deep sleep, troubled by images of a naked Rasputin and assuaged by those of an equally naked Irina. He woke up three hours later when the phone next to his bed rang and the receptionist told him that Oswald Rayner was waiting for him in the lobby and a package had been dropped off for him.

Chapter 18 – 1916 Petrograd

Don't allow concern to get in the way of opportunity

Rayner was sitting at a table in the corner drinking tea and eating smoked sturgeon on thin black bread. He had a wooden box next to him.

"Hope you don't mind me opening this," he said, handing Leon the box. "It's from Yusupov. The note said you won the wager."

Leon reached in and pulled out a yellow enameled container that looked like a clown hat.

Rayner noticed his confusion. "It's a bloody Fabergé piece. A Doge hat-shaped bonbonniere if I'm not mistaken. Those are rubies, emeralds, diamonds, and pearls. Worth an absolute fortune, you lucky beggar. What in God's name did you do to deserve that?"

"Not much," said Leon, rather annoyed at the sheer cheek of Rayner to open his package. "Just a night of frolicking with the Grand Duchess Vladimir. Game old bird."

"Good God," exclaimed Rayner, almost choking on his

sturgeon sandwich. "Do you mean...?" He didn't finish his question.

"Oh, most assuredly yes, and if I weren't so shagged out after the Duchess, I would have joined Rasputin and one of the Montenegrin princesses in a *ménage à trois.* Though it was a trifle hot in the *banya* for any serious activity."

"You devil," Rayner said with a large grin on his face. "My God, you've fitted into the scene perfectly. Rogering the Tsar's aunt the first night...who would have thought. Hmm, well, as intriguing as your encounter with Grand Duchess Vladimir sounds, I am more interested in your meeting with Rasputin. How the merry hell did you manage that?"

"Certainly not my doing," replied Leon, pouring himself a cup of tea and taking a sandwich. "If I'd arranged it, I promise you I'd have had my *sica* with me and your troubles with the Mad Monk would be over. No, the bastard kidnapped me on my way back to the hotel from the Vladimir Palace. But don't look so worried. He wants to meet with me again to coach me on what to say to my 'superiors' about why Russia must break the Triple Entente and seek an alliance with Germany. The man's nuttier than a fruitcake, though I can't say I disagree with some of his beliefs."

"You'd better fill me in," Rayner said, signaling a passing waiter to bring a bottle of vodka.

Half an hour later he sat back in his chair and folded his hands in front of him like a bishop praying. "Well, well. He most assuredly opened up to you. Some of what he said and some of his sentiments, if not already common knowledge, are suspected by Yusupov and the others, but there's a great deal I doubt if anyone other than you and the Montenegrins know. Who'd have thought that *asperine,* the supposed miracle drug, may have contributed to the Tsarevitch's issues?

"As far as the Black Princesses are concerned, Princess Anastasia told me, they simply don't care. They're only interested in the church and Rasputin's hideous cock."

Rayner blinked when Leon mentioned the monk's penis. "Hideous, you say? Then I wonder why he's much sought after by his female followers."

"Certainly wasn't his hygiene," said Leon. "Despite the *banya,* the man smelt like a goat. But I have to say I had some sympathy for his feelings about the Russian aristocracy."

"You're not going all communist on me, are you? If you are then I'll keep the Fabergé piece because you won't need it."

"Far from it," Leon replied, taking the box from the table and placing it next to his chair. "I imagine the Grand Duke is going to stiff me. He hasn't sent the sword he wagered. Looked like a bit of a scoundrel and has now shown himself to be one. No, it's just that some of the things Rasputin said made me realize how much suffering and bloodshed can be firmly placed at the feet of leaders who think nothing of sending a million men off to die so that they can stay in power."

"Rather naïve way of putting it," Rayner said. "It's been that way forever. *Theirs not to reason why, theirs but to do and die.* The rulers make the rules; those ruled simply obey them."

"Perhaps, but the people in power in Russia and Germany and Austria are there because they were born into powerful positions. Unlike their ancestors, who at least had to fight their way to the top."

"Yes, but that's not the case in America, which is why President Wilson is reluctant to send troops. The common people count. And it's not really the case in Britain either."

"Maybe not in America, but I'd argue that in Britain the ruling classes still call the shots."

"Call the shots, you say? Hmm, a rather descriptive idiom of war. Well, I can't argue with you in principle, but the fact is we have precious little time to get into political philosophy. From what I know, the Tsarina suspects that a contingency of her clan is planning mischief, and she's increased the guards who keep Rasputin safe. On the other hand her protection of Rasputin is lighting fires under more feet than ever. It's a bad situation, I fear. Even the newly reinstalled *Duma* are banging the anti-Rasputin drum like the blazes. The loudest of all its members, Vladimir Purishkevick—an awful bugger—made a rather inflammatory speech a few weeks ago which has more people riled up than ever before. So, time is now of the essence. And we need to establish a plan."

"I don't have a plan other than I'll do my best to take him out when next he sees me. So long as it's not naked in the *banya* again. Hard to hide the *sica* without your pants on."

"Yes, C. said you used a special weapon for your work, but he didn't say much about it. What precisely is a *sica*?"

"It's part of a long story which most people find hard

to believe. I'll tell it to you one day, but right now I think I might go and grab a few more hours of sleep. I have a feeling I may have another engagement tonight, and I'd like to be refreshed."

"Care to tell me who?" asked Rayner, leaning forward until Leon could smell the sturgeon on his breath.

"Not really. No offence, but I'm not sure it's any of your business."

"It bloody well is my business. Everyone you see. Everything you do is my business. We don't have time for games or insubordination."

"First, this is no game, Rayner. I came here to do a job, and as far as I'm concerned, I'm doing it. I wish it were as simple as *find 'em and stick 'em,* but it's not. My bedroom abilities are courtesy of the British Secret Service, and so far they have proved invaluable. Second, I must remind you that I am a freelancer. My family has a contract with the Secret Service, but it's not an employment contract, so I am by no means insubordinate. I need you and Bertie to back me up and get me in where I need help making contact. But that's it. I have no wish to antagonize you in any way, but I think it is important to establish the ground rules."

Rayner sat back and took a sip of his vodka. He regarded Leon carefully for a few moments and then nodded.

"Very well. As I said to you yesterday, I appreciate you being open and honest. And you're right, my interest in who your mysterious date is for tonight is more out of my own curiosity and to a lesser degree concern for you. I have a feeling I know who it is, but I shan't pry further today. I do think, though, that we should meet tomorrow and try to secure your opportunity with Rasputin. I am supposed to see Yusupov this evening and will try to get his views on what's going on with the Tsarina and any movement on Rasputin's part. I'll also try to convince him that if he's up to monkey business, he should get you involved."

"Yes, but do that subtly. He seems like a blabbermouth."

"Of course. Now give me back the ambassador's wife's brooch. She hasn't missed it so far, but she will, the old bat."

After a final slug of vodka and a sturgeon sandwich, Leon went back to his room and fell asleep. He woke up at six and was just wondering when Irina would make contact when there was a knock at his door. It was old Gregor with a note to say that a sleigh would be waiting outside the hotel at nine o'clock. It wasn't signed.

"Could you press my dinner jacket and be back at eight thirty to do my bowtie?" Leon asked Gregor, who took the crumpled suit, gave his perfunctory bow, and left Leon to contemplate how he'd fill the next few hours. A long, hot soak in the bath tub and half an hour of practice with the *sica* brought him to eight fifteen. After he'd dressed and strapped the *sica* to his left ankle, he sauntered down to the lobby where he saw Bertie in conversation with a man who could have been Rayner's brother.

"Ah, Leon, dear boy. Back at it again, I see. Surprised you have any oomph left after last night's performance. The Grand Duchess was raving about you when I saw her at lunch today. By the way, let me introduce you to Stephen Alley. He's one of us and knows everything."

"It seems everyone does. For members of the Secret Intelligence Service, you gentlemen have a hard time keeping a secret."

"Cheeky blighter, isn't he Stephen?' asked Bertie with a grin.

"Nice to meet you, Harries," said Alley, shaking Leon's hand. "I dare say you're right in your observation of our indiscretion. Under normal circumstances, we'd be a lot more hush-hush. But all of us in the Secret Service — Rayner, Bertie, me, and John Scale, who's in Romania now busy blowing up their oil fields to prevent the Huns from tapping them— are known to the Russians and Germans.

"Isn't that an issue? I mean doesn't the word 'secret' in Secret Service mean just that?"

Alley smiled. "In Petrograd these days, it's not about who you are but whom you're connected to Bertie has the ears of the Romanov family; both Rayner and I know Yusupov. You, it would seem, have made quite a stir in the few days you've been here. Don't get cocky, that's all."

Leon, who was definitely feeling "cocky," would dearly have loved to tell Alley to shove it. Instead, he nodded his head as if taking the advice seriously. He'd antagonized enough of C.'s agents over the years, and Alley had the appearance of someone who knew what he was talking about.

"I appreciate that," he said. "As C. has reminded me on many occasions, I tend towards insolence and presumption more often than is good for me. But I shall endeavor to be more diffident while here."

Both Bertie and Alley nodded.

"Now," Leon said, any trace of servility vanishing from

his tone, "I have an appointment with a lady, so I must be off. Toodle-oo. Nice to have met you, and I shall certainly need your help once I've accomplished what C. sent me here to do."

Had Leon not been so keen to rush out, he would have been given an urgent and hastily scribbled note sent to him by Rayner.

Urgent, it said. *Something is about to go down tonight at the Yusupov home. I know that's where you're headed, so please wait for further instructions. Do not go there under any circumstances.*

Chapter 19 – 1916 Petrograd

A most irregular evening with a Lady

Waiting for Leon outside the hotel was a small single-horse sled. The hotel doorman helped him in, covered him with the heavy blankets, and wished him a good night. The sled made its way through the ice-covered streets, which were eerily void of activity. It felt to Leon as if a funeral shroud had been thrown over the snow-covered city.

He reached down under the blankets to touch the *sica*, which, as always, gave him some comfort. He wasn't even sure why he'd brought it. There was little likelihood of him needing it in the Yusupov Palace that night. But he'd missed one opportunity early that morning because he'd left it behind, and he wasn't about to make the same mistake again.

When they came to the Moika River, the sled made a right turn past the carved wooden doors that served as the main entrance to the huge Yusupov Palace. It turned onto a side alley and stopped outside an open doorway, where a young maid stood shivering.

"Please to follow me, sir," she said in broken English as she quickly closed the door behind Leon. She led him down a long corridor, bare of both decoration and warmth, and so dimly lit that on his own, Leon would have fallen down the staircase if the maid hadn't stopped him in time.

"My God," he said under his breath. "You'd think they were wealthy enough to install decent lighting." He clung to the railing as they descended into yet another passageway, this one constructed of heavy stone. Leon's anxiety increased as they made their way along the barrel-vaulted tunnel that seemed to branch off in different directions. It felt very much like a trap.

The maid stopped at a glossy, red-painted door and knocked three times. Without waiting for a response, she opened it and let Leon into a well-lit and beautifully furnished room where Princess Irina Alexandrovna, only niece of Tsar Nicholas II and wife of the wealthiest man in Russia, Prince Felix Yusupov, reclined on a blue-velvet chaise in front of a roaring fire drinking a glass of champagne.

For a moment Leon gaped like a hooked fish at the stunning woman with dark hair and soft eyes who smiled up at him.

"Your Highness," he said, taking her proffered hand and kissing it. Horniness replaced nervousness and his kiss lingered, perhaps a little too long, before she withdrew her hand.

"Please," she said, indicating a chair to the side of the chaise. "Sit and I will have the maid pour you champagne—or vodka if you prefer. Are you hungry?"

Her voice was breathy, and Leon detected a shyness that only increased her appeal.

"Champagne will be perfect, and yes, Your Highness, I'm hungry, but not for food."

She giggled and lowered her eyes. "Good, because that is what I wish to engage you in this evening."

"I'm at your service," replied Leon, wondering if he should throw caution to the wind and undress right then and there. And he would have done so if the maid hadn't entered with a bottle of champagne and another glass. When she'd poured Leon's champagne and topped up the princess's, she whispered something to Irina, who raised her eyebrows and then left, closing the door behind her.

"A slight complication," said the princess. "It appears that my husband is expecting a guest down here in the basement."

"In this room?" asked Leon.

"No, in another part of the basement. But we shall have to be cautious so as not to bump into him when we are done. The problem is my husband thinks I am in the Crimea at one of our estates. I had to deceive him in order to see you."

"I appreciate that," said Leon, "but I'm not sure I feel all that comfortable knowing he is in the palace. What happens if he finds out we're together?"

"Do not concern yourself about that. He won't come in here—I very much doubt he is even aware of my private suite in this part of the basement—and none of my servants would dare to tell him that I never left Petrograd. Tomorrow I will tell him that I decided to come home early. Anyway, let us not spoil this evening with worry. Though, it is my husband's behavior that I wish to consult with you about."

"Indeed, Your Highness?" Leon was totally confused. He'd never heard a night of carousing referred to as a "consultation." Still, these aristocrats were all loony, and after the escapades at Schwerin Castle and his night with the Grand Duchess Vladimir, he was open to whatever she had in mind.

"Are you comfortable in the chair?" she asked.

"Quite, but I feel the chaise would better suit our purpose. I speak purely from experience. Chairs, no matter how comfortable, can be tricky."

"Forgive me, Leon, but I'm not sure I understand. I will be sitting here," she tapped the chaise with her hand, "and you will be seated in the chair. That should be perfect for our conversation. I really hope I have not given you the wrong impression. I would be so embarrassed."

It suddenly dawned on Leon—as it should have done earlier—that she really did mean a "consultation" in the accepted meaning of the word. He felt like a complete nincompoop with a large bruise forming on his ego.

"Oh no, Princess. There is no need to feel embarrassed. It is I who should feel shame. The seating arrangement is perfect. Now, please enlighten me as to what you wish to consult me on."

"Thank you," she said. "Well, it's a little discomfiting to talk about, but I am assured that there is no one more qualified than you in the subject." She paused, swallowed a large sip of champagne, and took a deep breath. "I need to understand the techniques that will entice my husband to my bed."

"Good Lord!" Leon gulped and then recovered. "Do you mean to say the bugger—I do beg your pardon, Princess—Prince Yusupov won't jump into bed with you? It's ludicrous! You're the most beautiful woman I've ever seen. He's not blind by any chance? Didn't seem to be at dinner last night."

"No, of course not. It's just that I think he is more comfortable with other men than with me."

Leon shook his head. "I am sorry to hear that, but what can I do?"

"You can show me ways that I can tempt him, make him desirous of my body. Tell me what you did with the Von Mecklenburg-Schwerin cousins that caused them to write such a glowing letter to the Grand Duchess?"

"Your Highness," Leon said, standing up and turning his back to the fire. "This is all very puzzling. While it's true that I did spend some intimate time with the Germans and the Grand Duchess last night, I find it hard to believe that they would have waxed elaborately about my techniques."

"I'm sure it is hard to imagine," said the princess, "but you have to understand that so many of the noble women in Europe are frustrated by their husbands who make love to them in order to procreate only. The rest of the time they spend with their mistresses, or in many cases with other men. Most of our marriages are arranged for power or money. Few for love."

"I understand. It sounds positively rotten, and you have my sympathy," Leon said, reaching over to pat her hand. "There, there, dear Princess Irina, do not fret. Why don't you unburden yourself about your husband, and while I'm no expert if his affections are for men, I will do what I can to help you. There are, of course, a few moves that I could share that may make a difference."

Princess Irina squeezed his hand in return, which sent a shiver up Leon's spine. "My husband is a complicated man. When he was much younger, he took great pleasure in scandal. He would go to balls dressed as a woman. He would carouse with men. Drink heavily, gamble. In fact, he loved to do all the things that make society gasp in horror. And yet, with all that, he is still the kindest of men. He has turned one wing of the palace into a hospital for the war wounded, and unlike many of the other aristocratic families, he believes in helping the poor."

"Yes, I heard about that, though judging by the way the person who told me reacted, it seems there's no satisfying the blighters."

"Yes, the peasants are always ungrateful for everything, but I don't wish to discuss the unfortunate state of Russia. I know the prince has a deep affection for me, and our time in bed together, as seldom as it may be, is extremely loving. Though when he leaves, he always seems unsatisfied. As am I, of course. My suspicion is that while he is attracted to both men and women, it is in the arms of men he is most happy. So, you can understand why I desperately want him to find me desirous. Please, tell me you can alleviate this void that fills our marriage."

"I see," said Leon, pinching his chin. "Well, this is a multifarious situation. But I shall do my best, Your Highness. Now, where should we begin?"[15]

---

[15] *Editorial interruption: As you've no doubt read by now—both in this book and the previous one, The Bodyguard of Sarawak—Leon is no stranger to gay men. And in all of these encounters, whether with his*

Leon thought he knew in which direction the staircase lay. After a few minutes of wandering down different corridors, he realized he was totally lost in the labyrinth of a basement in the palace on the Moika. He could see a faint light in the distance, and he followed it until he came to a door that was slightly ajar and from behind which he could hear the sounds of heavy breathing, grunting, and scuffling. He poked his head around the corner and saw Rasputin strangling Prince Yusupov.

---

great friend Philip Sassoon, Marcel Proust, or Bertie Stopford, he is neither judgmental nor critical. If anything, he is very accepting of them. The world then (as it is now) was fouled by the outrage of sanctimonious men and women who railed against homosexuality. Of course, it was illegal in most countries with horrendous punishments meted out to those who were caught in flagrante delicto. While there were great advances being made in the understanding of sexual adversity at the time, and to some small extent common people in England were more tolerant in their views of gay love it was highly unusual to discuss it in open conversation. Knowing Leon as I did in later life, I do remember him as having a "live and let live" attitude to most things. Though as a master assassin and rake extraordinaire, some may find his observations of morality highly questionable.

What Leon and Princess Irina discussed further and what occurred in the secret room in the bowels of the Yusupov Palace is not covered in his notes. But as you will momentarily discover, what happened in the princess's boudoir paled in comparison to what happened in another room not far away. It was an event so shrouded in lies, deceits, mystery, and mayhem that historians to this day don't know precisely what happened. Unless they've read this book, of course. Feel free to blab to any historians of your acquaintance, or better yet, get them to buy the book. The date was December 30th (17th in the old version of the Russian calendar) and the time 1:35 a.m. I can't work out why Leon left the princess's room on his own—perhaps the maid had gone to bed or perhaps he was looking for the bathroom.

Chapter 20 – 1916 Petrograd

Kill and overkill

The monk had his back to the door, and his hands were firmly clasped around the neck of the Prince, whose trembling feet were barely touching the floor as the life was choked out of him. There was an overturned chair and table, and a broken bottle of Madeira wine and small cakes were scattered on the carpet.

"Jesus!" shouted Leon.

For a second the monk froze. Then he let Yusupov fall to the floor and turned to face Leon. He snarled a short Russian phrase which Leon took to mean *now it's your turn, you bastard* or something that conveyed an equally barbarous threat and rushed at Leon, his hands out in front of him.

Rasputin stopped momentarily as Leon dropped into a crouch and rolled behind the monk. Then the monk's knees buckled, and he made a sound like air escaping from an inner tube as Leon plunged the *sica* into his liver. He attempted to turn his head to see what had happened as Leon slid the *sica* across to sever his hepatic artery.

Rasputin's blue eyes clouded over, and with his last breath he whispered to Leon in English, "I knew it would be you." Of course it could have been something in Russian that sounded exactly like that, but that's how Leon remembered it. Then Rasputin fell forward onto his face and lay still.

"Is he dead?" croaked Yusupov, who'd pulled himself up on a chair. His face had gone from a near-death blue to a very-much-alive angry red.

"I would say so," said Leon. "No one survives a poke in the liver with one of these." He cleaned the blade of the *sica* on Rasputin's pants and slid it back into its scabbard. He looked around at Yusupov and saw that the prince had a revolver in his hand. "Hey! What the hell are you doing?"

Before Leon could stop him, the prince shot Rasputin in the back, right above the stab wound. "Just making sure," said Yusupov. He bent down and, grabbing Rasputin by his left arm, he turned the body over. "Yes, he certainly looks dead, the swine." He gave the monk a vicious kick to the side of the head as if to emphasize his feelings and turned to Leon. "Help me get the body to the courtyard."

Leon had half a mind to tell the prince to do his own dirty work but thought better of it. He needed a reason to explain his presence in the palace, and this would give him a few minutes to think of one.

As they dragged the body along the corridor, back-breaking work for two people not used to manual labor, Yusupov said, "I really must thank you for saving my life. This devil would have strangled me. He was supposed to be dead from drinking the wine and eating the cakes which that idiot doctor supposedly laced with potassium cyanide."

Leon grunted, his mind still a blur of excuses for being in the palace, each sounding weaker than the previous. They dragged the body into the courtyard of the palace and the prince told Leon to wait while he got the others to help dispose of the corpse. Leon's first instinct was to run, but he realized it would have made it too easy for Yusupov to frame him if that was his intent. Better to be one of the conspirators than the lone killer.

He didn't have long to wait before Yusupov, Grand Duke Dmitri Pavlovich, and a man he didn't recognize but was introduced to him as the politician Vladimir Purishkevich rushed through the door into the courtyard. All were armed and to Leon's amazement, Purishkevich fired his revolver into Rasputin's back.

"He'd bloody dead," yelled Leon. "What's wrong with you people?" He watched in horror as the three men each gave the body a few sound kicks, and then the Grand Duke took aim with his pistol and shot Rasputin in the forehead. At which point Leon threw up.

"Who is this man?" asked Purishkevich, pointing his pistol at Leon.

"He is a friend of Bertie Stopford," Prince Yusupov said, "and he saved my life. That *muzhik* would have strangled me if this gentleman hadn't stabbed him. The poison had no effect on Rasputin."

"Oh, I meant to tell you," said Grand Duke Pavlovich almost casually, "Dr. Lazovert decided not to administer the cyanide. Said it was too obvious, or something to that effect."

The prince looked flabbergasted. "And that crucial detail is something you simply forgot? My God, a fine murderer you turned out to be." He shook his head in frustration and then turned to Leon. "The question is, what were you doing here tonight? Knowing your predilection, I would have said to sleep with my wife, but she of course is in the Crimea. Care to explain yourself?"

Before Leon could open his mouth—and it was fortunate because he still hadn't thought of an excuse—a figure stepped out from the shadows. "I sent him, and from what I've observed, he was just what the three of you needed."

"Rayner," said Yusupov, "I knew I could count on you." He walked up to Rayner, embraced him, and kissed him on both cheeks.

"And I asked you to wait for me," Rayner said, taking a step back. His voice though calm was tinged with anger. "Leon is a highly trained assassin working for the British Intelligence Service. I sent him here because I knew the three of you would bungle it, and it appears I was correct."

"Hold your tongue, sir," said Purishkevich angrily. "You are addressing an important member of the *Duma*, not to mention a Grand Duke and a Prince."

"I know precisely whom I am addressing," replied Rayner. "At the moment your status is irrelevant. You have just conspired to kill someone who is highly regarded by the Tsarina and the Tsar. In this matter your titles are meaningless. Now, my suggestion is you get rid of the body as best you can. Gather up some chains and a sheet and throw him into the river, but not right in front of the palace. Leon, you'd better go with them to see it all goes smoothly. Once you're done, return to the hotel and we'll get you out of here."[16]

---

[16] *Editorial interlude: The events that transpired at the Yusupov Palace on the night of December 29th and the morning of December 30th are still highly speculative and often contradictory. There are numerous accounts written by those involved (all suffered no more than a slap on the wrist for their part) but the best—and certainly most comprehensive—exposé can be found in Margarita Nelipa's incredibly well-researched book, Killing Rasputin: The murder that Ended the Russian Empire. Ms. Nelipa is a medical scientist with postgraduate legal qualifications, both of which give her a unique insight into actual murder and events that led up to it. She talks at length of the involvement of the British Intelligence Agency, and while she believes they were aware of the plot, they were not involved in the actual killing itself. I found a few accounts that suggest Rayner participated, but Ms. Nelipa vehemently denies it. In fact, the only reference I could find to Leon's participation in the murder of Rasputin (other than his notes) was in a cable sent by German agents in Stockholm to Berlin. The agents claimed they had it on good authority that a "young Englishman" had been in the Yusupov Palace that night. Another secret communique to the King of Bulgaria (of all people) placed an Englishman who fitted Leon's description in the car that took the body of the monk to the Petrovskii Bridge that crossed towards Krestovsky Island, where the conspirators disposed of Rasputin's corpse into the icy river. The two people who knew the truth were Rayner and Yusupov. Rayner couldn't admit it and Yusupov didn't care to. Oh, there's one more bit of circumstantial evidence that gives some credence to Leon's account of the events surrounding Rasputin's death. Both Prince Felix and Princess Irina Yusupova escaped from Russia and eventually moved to Paris, where they remained happily married for more than fifty years. Clearly the techniques that Leon had taught Irina that fateful night proved to be highly effective. Well, I like to think so.*

Chapter 21 – 1916 London

Just when you thought it was over

Captain Hugh Sinclair of the *Renown* seemed pleased to see Leon. "Nice coat," he said, admiring Leon's Astrakhan. Once again Leon had had no opportunity to pack. Rayner had met him in the lobby of the hotel when the Grand Duke dropped him off after they'd dumped Rasputin's body into the Little Nevka river. The only item he handed Leon was the Fabergé bonbonniere. "Take this," he'd said. "You definitely earned it." Then he'd driven Leon, still in his crumpled formal attire, out of Petrograd to the bay where the naval launch had originally set him ashore.

"That was well done, old boy," Rayner said as he wished Leon goodbye. "I very much doubt your involvement and my presence will ever be fully exposed. But luckily for us you missed my note to stay back at the hotel, or God knows what would have happened. Yusupov would be dead, Rasputin very much alive, and the Grand Duke would probably have shot Furishkevich in the arse."

"Thank you, Oswald," Leon said, taking Rayner's hand. "I wish all C.'s men were as decent as you. Perhaps we'll see each other when this war is over."

"You'd better give my steward your shirt," said Sinclair.

Leon looked down at his dress shirt and saw that it was splattered with Rasputin's blood.

"Hopefully that blood isn't yours?"

"Oh, no," replied Leon, taking a sip of the scotch and soda that Sinclair's steward had handed him when he'd entered the captain's cabin. "It's the other bloke's." He gave a laugh that sounded nervous but had more to do with exhaustion.

"You certainly work fast," Sinclair said. "It's only been three days since we dropped you off. I trust you were successful?"

"I did what I came to do. So, hopefully. But you never know, do you?"

"No, you don't. Unlike Newton's predictable Third Law, in war as opposed to motion—or at least it's been my experience—every action, no matter how trivial and insignificant, has a reaction that is usually so incalculable we have absolutely no way to control it. I have some idea of what your mission was. If you were successful, as you say, and I don't doubt you for a bit, it may keep Russia as our allies...and then again it may bring down the entire Russian empire sooner than we imagined. Whatever the outcome, it was well worth the risk."

Leon nodded. He wasn't sure what made sense anymore. He thought back to how many "enemies of the state" he'd killed over the previous five years, all either to help stop the war from happening or to help the allies win. And yet as he looked back, the war was most definitely happening; millions had been killed, and it was still up in the air whether the allies could even win. Especially if the Americans didn't lend a hand. Perhaps, as Captain Sinclair put it, everything he'd done was well worth the risk, but it was unclear whether the risk had paid off at all.

There was no Frank Barnwell waiting in Kirkwall to fly him home in his Bristol, but the captain of a fast scout cruiser on its way to the Deptford Royal Dockyard for repairs offered him passage.

"Such a lovely coat," said his mother when he walked into the Sir Sydney Smith shortly after he'd disembarked. "Where did you get it...Liberty?"

"Actually, no," Leon replied, giving his mother a kiss. "I got it in St. Petersburg or Petrograd, as it's now called."

His mother shook her head. "St. Petersburg? When were you there?"

"A couple of days ago. I just got back."

"Impossible," said his father, who'd been fixing one of the beer tap handles that had come loose. "You were here six or seven days ago. You can't go that far and back in such a short time."

"You can if you fly halfway on a plane and the do the rest on a fast naval ship."

"You went on a plane? My God, you could have been killed," Bryna said, ringing her hands.

"Trust me," replied Leon, "flying was the very least of the dangers." He told them about the Princes and Grand Dukes, Bertie Stopford and Oswald Rayner, and his part in the death of Rasputin.

"You realize," said Abraham, "the Okhrana could easily have found out who you really were. They still have a price on my head from the time I left them to work for the British."

"Oh, I doubt they'd have had much time to worry about me with the country on the brink of revolution. Of course, that may change if they ever find Rasputin's body. In which case I'd better hope that Yusupov and Pavlovich still want to take credit. I'm sure they will. Those sorts can't stand to see anyone else in the limelight."

"Did the Grand Duchess have wonderful jewelry?" asked Bryna, changing the subject.

"She did, which reminds me…." He took the Fabergé bonbonniere out its box and showed it to his parents.

"My God, this must be worth a fortune," Abraham said as he examined the exquisite container. "Maybe you should show it to your friend Philip. He probably collects Fabergé."

"You didn't steal it, did you?" asked his mother, looking suspiciously at her son.

"Mama," Leon replied, shaking his head. "Have you ever known me to steal anything? I'm an assassin not a thief. No, I won it in a bet with Prince Yusupov, but trust me—you don't want to know what the wager was all about."

She snorted. "You're right. I don't want to know."

His father gave him a wink. "I do, but you'll tell me over

a drink later. Now, off you go to meet with Smith-Cumming."

Leon had to wait more than an hour for C. to return to his office at 2 Whitehall Court from a meeting with the newly appointed British Prime Minister, David Lloyd George.

"Sorry to have kept you, my boy," said C. cheerfully. "Had to brief the new man. Nice coat by the way. Did we buy it for you?"

"Yes, and if you want it back, you'll need to send it to the cleaners. Probably still has some of Rasputin's grey matter on it."

C. waved off Leon's offer with a smile. "No, you can keep it. You did a good job according to Rayner. Hoare's a little miffed he wasn't in on it, and Ambassador Buchanan will have to convince the Tsar that no British agents were involved. But all in all, a success. Yusupov and his chums will have to take responsibility as they rightly should."

"I hope the Russian generals are better at strategy and execution than those idiots," Leon said.

"I very much doubt it. The Russians are useless friends but dangerous enemies. And as allies in the war against the Hun, let's just say their abilities are questionable. But they're all we have so far until the Americans make up their damn minds whether they're in or out. Perhaps Lloyd George will do a better job of convincing Wilson than Asquith ever did. Of course, that's if they can understand the man. Do you know that English is his second language? Blighter grew up speaking Welsh. Who'd have thought we'd have a Welshman as PM?"

"Hopefully his wife prefers him to a sheep," Leon said, thinking of the insult Prince Yusupov had flung at him.

"What the bloody hell are you talking about?" asked C. "His wife prefers sheep?"

"Oh, just something stupid I heard in Petrograd. Think nothing of it."

"Humph," C. said, looking at Leon as if he were mad. "Well, it appears his head's in the right place, at least, which is more than I can say for yours today. I do feel bad for Asquith losing out like that. Like him a lot. Thought he was a good PM...but that's politics for you, as they say."

Much to Leon's annoyance—though he did his best to hide it—C. went into one of his diatribes on the intrigues of the political parties until his secretary knocked on the door.

"Your next appointment will be here in five minutes, sir."

"Oh, do tell the bugger to wait so I can finish with young Harries here."

"I'm not sure I could tell Major General Edgerton to wait, sir."

"Probably not; the man's a tyrant when he's happy and unspeakable when he's not. Okay, Leon, I'll be quick. I need you to go back to Africa."

"I thought we'd driven the Germans out of South West Africa?"

"That's true; the South Africans mopped up that part of the world, but your old nemesis Von Lettow-Vorbeck is still causing havoc in East Africa. You are leaving for Dar es Salaam to meet with the South African General Jan Smuts. He's a brilliant man, but he could use your special skills."

At that moment they were interrupted by a booming voice. "I don't give a fiddler's if he's still tied up. Tell him I'm here and I don't have time to wait."

The secretary poked her head round the door. "General Egerton is here and—"

C. put up his hand. "Yes, we heard. Good luck, Leon, my boy. Miss Ramsey here can give you the details for your trip. Don't bloody stab Egerton on your way out, will you. We need him."

It is at this point that the 2nd part of Leon's diary found sewn into the back of the final volume of The Haji Baba saga ends. I have no clue as to whether he made it to Dar es Salaam and met with the great General Smuts or not. Perhaps some relative somewhere—and once again, they're scattered around the globe like raisins in a fruitcake, just as they were after escaping the pogroms in Lithuania and Belarus in the 1880s—will find his notes detailing what happened. All I do know is that at some time between when he left C.'s office and the beginning of World War II, he returned the sica to my grandfather Joe, who passed it on to my father. As I said in the beginning of The Bodyguard of Sarawak, Leon resembled neither a master assassin nor a great lover, and yet he was both.

Post Script

I always wondered what became of the Fabergé bonbonniere that Leon won from Prince Yusupov the night before he killed Rasputin. I asked my relatives, but no one had even heard of it (or if they had, they were keeping it to themselves). Then my younger son Steve sent me a screenshot from a Christie's auction catalogue where "a jeweled and enamel gold bonbonniere in the form of a doge's hat by Fabergé, St. Petersburg 1899-1904" was listed as having been sold for one hundred and sixty-two thousand, five hundred pounds. Provenance was listed as "anonymous sale." Clearly someone was lying, though knowing my family, it shouldn't come as too much of a surprise.

The end.

Acknowledgements

Thanks to my wonderful editor, agent, and friend Melissa Mazzeo. I can't imagine writing these books without her. To Luis Dias, a friend and colleague for so many years who graciously and wonderfully comes up with ideas for the cover. To Brenda and my family in Australia for always reading and rarely criticizing, and my sons Simon and Steve and their wives Tracey and Lisa for doing the same. To my wife Jennifer, who puts up with my blank stares when she asks me something and my mind is focused elsewhere, most likely on the murder of some malevolent character. And finally, to my great-uncle Leon. If only half the things he told me were true he'd have lived a life few others have or have ever imagined.

A note from the author

Thank you so much for reading my book. I hope you enjoyed reading it as much as I enjoyed writing it. If you liked the book, I would be so appreciative if you would take a moment to leave a review for me on Amazon. Since I am new to writing and publishing, every review counts. And since all of my book sales are donated to animal charities, I know the animals will thank you as well.

Please also check out my FREE starter library, including short story Death by Green Monkey and full-length novel Infatuation, only at www.jonathanharriesink.com

Thirty-five years before the fateful reunion with Freddy Blank in Paris, Roger Storm was living into Johannesburg—and his larger-than-life friends are already getting him into trouble! Check out Roger Storm's first brush with a near-death experience, totally free at my website!

INFATUATION
A NOVEL OF QUESTIONABLE TASTE
BY JONATHAN HARRIES

How far would you go for love at first sight? When Charley Brooks catches a glimpse of the voluptuous belly dancer Fanny Packer by chance in a magazine, forces beyond reason lead him to set aside his life in New York City with his perfect fiancée to chase the woman of his dreams. A mysterious book, a homicidal dwarf, a dominatrix, and a brothel on wheels all feature in this love story on acid that finds Fanny and Charley in each other's arms in this life–and maybe even into the next one.

Also by Jonathan Harries

The Roger Storm Books

KILLING HARRY BONES
BY JONATHAN HARRIES

Roger Storm, drinking heavily and contemplating suicide after his divorce and unceremonious firing from a high-powered job, gets the shock of his life when he meets his childhood friend, Freddy Blank, years after his supposed death. Roger soon finds himself dragged kicking and screaming into an adventure where a mysterious international organization is taking out poachers and trophy hunters in precisely the same ways they take out animals. Don't miss this hugely inventive, action-packed, hilarious debut novel from Jonathan Harries!

KILLING BOBBY FATT AND OTHER NASTY BASTARDS.
BY JONATHAN HARRIES

Roger Storm is back in this thrilling second book in the series! The bucolic peace of Hunter's Folly Private Game Reserve is shattered by the discovery of a noseless hunter next to a hornless rhino carcass, sending Roger on another mad adventure helping his friends to take down one of the most vicious animal trafficking rings in the world—and helping the animals to fight back!

On a remote hunting preserve in Namibia, a brilliant Indian geneticist is facing a rather nasty end unless he can find a way for elephants to grow longer tusks, rhinos bigger horns, and lions thicker manes. Behind this dastardly scheme is the notorious Russian oligarch Valerian Zolotov and members of *Bratva*, the Russian mafia. But there's an equally dangerous group determined to save the geneticist and put a permanent stop to these rotters.

Tales of the Sica

I had absolutely no intention of getting into the family business. As I told my father the night he enlightened me on what my ancestors had been up to for over a thousand years, "Sticking a curved dagger into someone's liver ain't quite my cup of tea." As it turned out, I had no choice. When your family's been assassinating reprobates and other loathsome individuals for seventy generations, you have a certain obligation.

Can you blame a chap for wanting to turn his otherwise humdrum family into a bunch of assassins? It turns out you can. I found this out soon after my novel The Tailor of Riga was published, and I received a bunch of beastly emails and threats from incensed family members horrified that I'd portrayed them as the descendants of bloodthirsty hitmen. Then, out of the blue, a package arrived from a long-lost cousin in Argentina that changed everything.

When the British Secret Service Bureau commissioned my great-uncle Leon to whack a Russian Count aboard the SS Gwalior on its way from Cape Town to Mombasa, he had no idea the size of the maelstrom into which he was about to plunge. After tossing out bodies to the lions of Tsavo in Kenya, graduating with honors from a school specializing in sexual techniques in Singapore, avoiding headhunters in the sweltering jungles of Sarawak, to becoming bodyguard to his highness Charles Brooke, the 2nd Rajah of Sarawak, Leon carves a magnificent swath of death and seduction as the 68th generation in our family assassination business. Read now!

About the Author

I grew up in Namibia, an extraordinarily beautiful and wild country where the desert meets the sea, with not a blade of grass in between. In my early teens we moved to South Africa where, after completing the perfunctory exercises necessary for entering adulthood, I began a career in advertising. While my love and fascination with wildlife began in Namibia, it grew into a passion in South Africa, and I spent every chance I got going to Botswana and other places where you could—and luckily still can—see animals in their natural habitat.

I moved to the US in 1986 because it didn't seem as if apartheid would ever end, and I've lived here ever since. I retired just over a year ago as Chairman of FCB, a global advertising agency, and published my first book, *Killing Harry Bones*. Both my sons are passionate about animals; my elder son, Simon, moved back to South Africa for a few years to become a safari guide. My wife and I go on safari as often as possible and have had some incredible trips into the bush, bringing back memories rather than trophies.

—Jonathan